A Classy
THUG

a Classy THUG

By

J.J. Jackson

Felony Books, a division of Olive Group, LLC,
P.O. Box 1577, Belton, MO 64012

ISBN-13: 978-1-940560-44-1

Felony Books 1st edition July 2017

10 9 8 7 6 5 4 3 2 1

Manufactured in the United States of America

For information regarding special discounts for bulk purchases, please contact Felony Books at felonybooks@gmail.com.

Books by J.J. Jackson:

O.P.P.
O.P.P. 2
O.P.P. 3
REVENGE IS BEST SERVED COLD
REVENGE IS BEST SERVED COLD 2
SCANDALS OF A CHI-TOWN THUG
HELL HAS NO FURY

www.felonybooks.com

Chapter 1
Deja

"This sun is blazing hot, at the same time it feels so good to just be outside getting some fresh air, don't it baby?"

"It sho do," my daughter says, gulfing down her ice cream cone.

"I just got off the phone with your uncle. I need to slide past his way then we can go to the mall, baby girl. Your father gave me some extra money. Now what you think about that?" I ask her as we sit on the porch of our house located in Oxon Hill, Maryland.

My 15-year-old child glances at the sky. "That sounds good. Maybe we can meet up with daddy too!" She's so excited about shopping.

"Not today. I just want it to be girl's day out. How about we get our nails and feet done? What you got to say to that?"

"Ok!" she voices all excited, getting up to go in the house.

The both of us enter the house, gather our things for our day together. We don't get to be together much because her father and I go out of town a lot. She stays with her auntie most of the time. It's like she's her auntie's child and not mines but all that is about to change. Me and Zac are going to have a heart to heart 'cause I feel we brought her in this world so we need to take care of her ourselves.

"You ready, momma?" she asks, standing at the door all dolled up wit' her little purse.

"Since I was born little girl let's roll."

We get in the car, turn up the sounds, put our shades on and roll out.

Chapter 2
Nikki

Me and my mother have the top dropped to her new Benz my father bought her. We're cruising on the highway. We been shopping all day just doing some girly stuff. I glance at the sky, thinking of my grandmother. I miss her so much. She used to always take me to do stuff like this. Not that I'm not happy today being with my mother. All in all it turned out to be a good day. I admire my mother, who's bobbing her head to B.I.G's "What's Beef?"

"Mom, thanks. It's just so nice out, the sun is shining so bright. I can't believe it's September. It's just so hot out."

"I know righ—"

Bang!

The jerk of her car cuts my mother short! We both look back.

"What in the hell?! I know he didn't just hit my car!" she hollers out.

Bang!

Again, he rams into my mother's car!

She pulls over to the curb. The two men jump out their car, running up to us with guns in their hands.

"Oh shit, they gon' kill us!" my mother yells as she mashes the gas, pulling off doing like 150 mph.

I'm scared as heck, trying not to cry. I keep looking back to see if the men are getting closer.

"Call your father! Call him now!" she yells while driving.

"Ok, ok!" I answer nervously, pulling out my phone, hitting speed dial for my dad. It goes straight to voice mail, I keep calling and calling only to get the same dang on results.

Spinning my head over at my mother, she's moving this car fast—I mean she is *getting it.*

"Ok, Nikki, I'ma pull over at the next light. You jump out and run and keep trying to get your father. Do not—I mean *do not*—call the police by any means, do you hear me?!"

"No!" I raise my voice. "No! I won't do it, mom. No, I'm not leaving you!"

"Nikki, right now ain't the fuckin' time!" she shouts, examining her surroundings. She notices the all black Jag is gaining speed.

She makes a sharp turn, pulling up to the shopping center.

"Now jump! Go!" she yells, spit flying out of her mouth.

I hesitate.

"I can't move. My legs, they won't move, ma!"

"Nikki, go get out!" She pushes me out the car. My body hangs halfway out.

"Keep calling your father, not the police. Remember what we taught you. If the police come, give them the name and address we told you. Now get!" She gives me one kick and my whole body falls out. I roll over and start running, looking up the road to see how close that Jag is getting to my mother. I start yelling, "Help, somebody help!"

I run in the Giant Food store, trying my daddy one more time. Still no answer.

"Fuck it!" I yell nervously. Hell I'm only fifteen and I don't wanna die. I don't want my mother to die.

"911, what's your emergency?"

"Hello, it's my mother ... somebody is trying to kill her."

"Where is she?"

"She's driving down 301 in a silver Benz and the man is in a black sports Jag!"

"I have it. Are you safe?"

"Yes, I think so. I'm in the Giant Food store on 301!"

"Ok, I'm sending someone for you. Where do you live?"

"1645 Walter Front Dr. Potomac, MD!"

"Is there an adult around you?"

"Yes, people … people … they are all around me now!"

"Ok, stay calm. It'll be ok. Help is on the way to your mom and you," the operator assures.

"I hear the helicopter. Is that for my mom?" I franticly ask.

"Yes, they can see her and the other car."

I hear sirens getting closer to me.

"You still there?" the lady asks.

"Yes."

This police woman walks up to me. "Are you ok?"

I look at her, shivering. "Yes, but my mother—how, where is she?"

"We have her. It's going to be ok."

After I hear those words I collapse in the officer lady's arms. I'm tired, scared and mad. I almost lost my mother over a car accident.

Chapter 3

Zec

"Zec, that feels so good *um* ... baby, you such a gentleman. I love you so much, dang baby. *Um ... yes,* right there," April moans, swaying her hips to the movement of my tongue as I hold on to her tender thighs, eating this pretty pussy. "Z, I'm cumming baby. It's cumming! It's running in your mouth, baby! Shit, Z!" she chants, shivering like the wind just blew through the house.

I lift my head, run my tongue up the center of her body, stopping at her lips, kissing them softly. She rolls on top and rides my dick like the cow girl she is. After about 10 strokes I nut all in her.

"That's what I'm talkin' 'bout, baby. Give it to yo man."

She examines my body like she wanna say, *What was that ol' half a minute shit?*

"Hell, I can't help it. Your pussy shouldn't be so damn good," I utter with a smile.

"That's ok. You make up for it with that tongue."

"I know," I shoot, loving on her with kisses.

"Z, why we still wearing condoms? We been together as long as you and Deja."

"News flash: I don't want no more kids. I didn't want the one I got, but she here so I gotta deal with it, right?" I turn over on the pillow, not wanting to get into this conversation.

"It's not fair," she pouts.

"Here we go." I get up so I can do a disappearing act in like 30 minutes. Going to the bathroom I hit the shower button, hop in while she complains about me not giving her a child.

"April, we been through dis like over and over right. The way I see it if you wanna be wit another dude, you gotta do you. I'll vanish, then the two of you can have like the Brady Bunch and shit."

"I know yo ass ain't just say dat. We been together since like 10th grade, when you ain't have shit in your pocket. Now you wanna get jazzy about my emotions? Fuck you and Deja. Y'all both can pass go straight to hell. Y'all meant for each other for real! I can get paid with my face, these hips and my ass. A bitch can make some money no problem in that department," she flexes.

"A'ight, I gotta go. I'll call you later. Let me know what strip club you at. I'll come throw you some ones and shit." I grin.

"So you Steve Harvey now? You got jokes? I got you. One day my ass gon' be out of sight, watch."

"If I watch then you won't be out of sight." I grin again. She throws a pillow at me. "What you want a nucca ta say, April? You not going nowhere. I got shit ta take care of. I been MIA since Monday. That's been two days now. I ain't even answered my phone, all outta respect for you. This the thanks you give me knowing I got a family, so right now I gotta jump ship."

"Whateva. When I'ma see you again?"

"Friday. I'll be back then. Talk to you lata," I voice, walking out the door.

"It's like that? I can't get a damn kiss?"

"Girl, you gon' drive a nucca crazy for real." I go back to the room, kiss her on the forehead.

"April, I'll see you Friday. I know it's hard. This what I'ma do, I'ma buy you a dog."

"Z, fuck you for real."

"When you do, I hope it's like you did today."

She throws another pillow. I run to the door, making my getaway.

Stepping to my truck, I hop in and flip my glove compartment open expediently retrieving my cell. I search through my messages.

"Daddy, Daddy, it's momma! Daddy, some men they got guns they tryna kill us daddy please answer!"

17

"Shit, my daughter my wife they in trouble when was this?" Checking the date: "Damn, that was yesterday fuck!" I start up my truck, call my sister as I back out of April's driveway mad as fuck.

"Dollar!"

"Yo, what happened to my daughter?!"

"Nutten, she's with me. She's ok, but don't be mad. She called the police. They got Deja."

"What? Why she do that? She knows bedda."

"Don't fuss at her she's only 15. Besides the fact two men was chasing your wife she was scared she didn't know what to do. You wasn't answering your phone, she said."

"What precinct is Deja in?"

"Seven D."

"DC?"

"Her car flipped as soon as she crossed the line."

"The car flipped? Why she in jail? She ok?"

"She had 10 white T shirts for the cook out."

"What? What she doing wit that small shit? What the fuck? Let me talk to Nikki."

"Nikki, your father's on the phone?" my sister Brandy calls out.

"Hi, daddy. It was horrible, it was horrible. But momma is ok. I know you mad at me but I didn't know what else to do, daddy. I just didn't ... I didn't want them men to kill my

18

momma. I only get one momma, daddy, and I didn't want her to be like grandma and leave me." She gives all the facts in one breath.

"Baby girl, I'm not mad at you. I just need to know what happened."

"Me and momma was in her Benz. These two men bumped us. Momma pulled over, they got out their car with guns. Momma mashed the gas, we was flying daddy. She pulled over at the shopping center then kicked me out, telling me to go to safety. She said to call you but you didn't answer my call so I had to call the police."

"What kind of car was the men in?"

"A black sport Jag."

"Did you see their faces?"

"No they had on hoodies, as hot as it was."

"You did good. I love you. I'll be past there lata. Put your auntie back on."

"Here, he wants to talk back to you."

"Brandy, I'll be past there tomorrow. In the meantime I'ma go to the station to see Deja. If she calls you tell'a I'ma call to get the visit times then I'll be there."

"Got you. You know Nikki's good."

"I know. Is my men over there?"

"Yeah, two in front and three in back as always."

"Good. I'll call you lata, sis."

"OK. Z?" she calls my name.

"I know. I'ma be careful, don't worry. I got me. One," I voice.

"One," she retorts.

All that runs through my mind is who would try me. *Who?!*

Chapter 4

Errica

"Hey girl, did you hear about Mr. Harris?" I lay it out in stone, standing in the doorway of her cell. "They say he was walked off."

"No say? I wonder why," my girl Dada spits.

"Don't know but he looked wired anyway. Did you call your sister yet?"

"Hell no. That bitch be lying, talking 'bout she put money on my books. That was yesterday. I know Western Union don't take one whole day ta post my money. I don't know why she be lying," Dada says, sitting on her bunk fired up.

"I know. I hate that shit too."

"Hey ladies," Officer Thompson creeps up to us.

"Hi, Mrs. Thompson," we spit in unison.

"What y'all up to?" the CO questions, observing the room like we got some contraband and shit.

"Mrs. T, you always be looking around the room. What you looking fo'? Ain't nobody got nutten," I speak up.

She smiles. "You never know."

"You know us, Mrs. T. We not the ones," Dada injects.

"No, I don't. Half the time I don't know myself, so keep it clean 'cause I ain't got time to be writing no shots," she states, forming her hand into a gun. We laugh. She creeps on. We continue to talk.

"Oh, I know what I wanted to tell yo ass." Dada waves her hands, signaling for me to come all the way in her room.

"What?" I whisper.

"You know Rekey? Girl, she got caught last night in the bathroom with that stud."

"What stud?"

"You know the one in K7."

I start thinking, *Stud in K7?* "You mean Mercy, the one with the two teeth hanging out her mouth?"

"Yeah, yeah. Girl, they was butt naked. They caught them fucking. Mercy was on her knees."

"Whaaa …! Who caught'em? I got a good idea."

"Mrs. Cox ass! Who else."

"They should've known bedda than ta been doing shit on her shift anyways. She got eyes in the back of her head."

"That's what I said."

"I got a bone to pick with yo ass, Errica," this trif' bitch stands outside Dada's cell door summoning me. Turning, I put on my nice face.

"Only dogs pick bones," I return.

"Dat right there is the shit I be talking 'bout. Now if I haul off and slap the shit outta yo—"

"I can see you doing a lot of shit but slapping me not one of'em." I stare her dead in her face.

"Anywho, did you tell Gatus I wanted ta fuck'a?"

"If the shoe fit try the muthafucka on." I get all in her space, daring this bitch ta even look like she gon' swing.

"Why would you tell her that?" she shoots back, keeping her voice to a minimum.

"Last time I looked, this tongue"—I stick it out in her face—"is mines to do what the fuck I wanna do wit'it," I remind her ass.

"And that same tongue can be snatched the fuck out yo mouth."

This bitch is tryin' me fo'real.

I step even closer, so close I can smell her nasty breath, so she can hear me loud and clear.

"Like I said, I see you doing much but not touching na part of my body that ain't one of'em. Even though I know you want to," I tell'a, grittin' on her punk ass running my hands down my sexiness.

"Bitch, I've fucked bitches like you on a humbug for free."

"Try to cash that ticket then you bad," I calmly deliver while she's yelling, getting off her square.

"Ladies, break it up or you will be sitting on the lieutenant's bench." Mrs. T starts walking up the hall spitting.

"Saved by the bell bitch," I tell her ass like somebody scared of her fat dike ass.

"Bathroom after 4 o'clock count, you so bad," she mumbles under her breath.

"Why put off at 4 what we can do now?" I smile as I deliver the blow.

"Come on, Errica, all she gon' do is tongue box," Dada interjects.

"I'm winning at that too," I tell Dada, eyeing her ass. Not wanting Mrs. T ta give me a shot, I back up into Dada's cell, putting my hand up to my neck in a knife formation running it across my throat.

"You wanna play 5,000?" Dada challenges as she sees Mrs. T walking up to her cell.

"Don't have the time. My man supposed to be here in a few."

"Oh bitch you didn't tell me Andrew was coming. Get some feels in for me."

"Will do. Let me go and get ready. It's not Andrew, it's Carton, my new man," I add.

"Ain't no feels gon' be happening nowhere," says Mrs. T. "If I here you two fussing again, y'all going down the hill. I told you to keep it clean on my shift. Mrs. Pratt, I ain't got time for paper work. I'll make you pay myself."

A *Classy* THUG

Mrs. T is one of the coolest officers around here. She don't mess wit' nobody. She keeps to herself. She's like one of those *you don't bother me I won't bother you* type officers, and we love it. But if you get her wrong she'll have no problem showing you she's the Head officer in charge. She leaves us be.

"What color lipstick you wearing?" Dada quizzes.

"Red, bright hoe ass red," I throw back.

"I hear dat hoe bitch."

"And you know I am." I smile as I flee back to my cell, thinking about that trif' bitch and how I'ma hav'ta slice bread wit'a. *You gotta show them just what 'hood you rep sometimes'.*

Chapter 5
Deja

I sit in the visiting room waiting for Zec. The CO told me he was here to see me.

"Whoo, who in the hell is that? His ass is fine as shit," one of the girls affirm out loud as my man enters the visit room.

"Them shoes had to cost like some thousands for real," another one comments.

I wave Zec over 'cause the room is so crowded. He pimp shuffles his cool ass over to my table.

"Hey, D, how it do?" is the first thing that comes out his mouth.

"I'm hanging," I tell him, giving him an old fashion peck on the mouth, scanning and watching all the women watching my man.

We sit down.

"You want anything from the machines?"

"No, you doing enough just by being here. Plus I'm full."

"What's that suppose ta mean, I'm doing enough? I can't help it if I'm sexy and fine at the same time."

"Boy, you so conceded."

"No it's confidence," he spits, rubbing the soft skin of his face, licking his sexy full lips.

My underwear starts to get creamy knowing what them lips can do.

Leaning back in his seat stretching his long legs: "On a serious note, what's the number for bail?"

"They didn't set it yet," I yawp.

"What you mean they didn't set it yet? Wuss up wit' that shit?"

"The lawyer said my hearing is Monday," I stress.

"So they saying you gotta stay in here over the weekend before them goof balls set bail. That's some real live bullshit."

"I say the same thing, but it's a waiting game. What can I do?" I blurt.

"Next question: Why in the fuck was you carrying that small shit? And where did you get powder from anyway?" he lets out cool, calm and collective as always.

"From James."

"What you doing fuckin' wit' that nucca without consulting with me? D, you know bedda."

"You right. But my brother needed it. He owe some people since you wouldn't front him the money. I thought he could put in his own work."

He sits up. I have his undivided attention now. "That crackhead muthafucka, I just fronted dat nigga 20G's two days ago. You got played by yo' own fam. I told you to only trust me, nobody else just yo man. What happened to that, bae? C'mon work wit a nucca."

"I'm sorry, I messed up Z. He's my brother. I believed him. What you want me to say?"

"I want you to say you gots to be mo careful, not you sorry. Sorry weighs heavy. We talked about this before, right? Now look—you got yo'self in a fucked up pickle. Now what you gon' do?

"I guess I gotta do the time."

"Dat shit sound good but you talking about being in these white folk cage wit' some ruthless killas, bae. You not built for that shit."

"I live wit one, Z," I tell his ass, gunning him down wit' his own hypothesis.

"Ok, you got me there."

"Do you know why them men was following me?" I demand an answer.

"First of all, let's change that. They not men by far. Men don't gun for women. No, I don't know who they are but when I find out you know I'ma dress they asses up."

"Z, how can you be so damn level-headed right now? Your woman is in here. I almost got killed and your daughter experienced it."

"What you want me ta do, cry? Yell? That shit ain't gon' do shit ta help madders. You still gon' be in here and it won't change the fact that our child got caught up," he explains.

Sighing, I ask, "How is Nikki doing?"

"She holding on. I'ma hit my sister's spot once I leave here. D, help me understand one thing: Why you ain't call one of my men to go with y'all?"

"I wanted to spend some time wit' Nikki alone. Just some girl time."

"So you couldn't do that shit with them in the background? She wouldn't even have known they was around. C'mon, D, you put our daughter in jeopardy for real, plus you was dirty."

"You right. I fucked up."

"Fuck *saying* the words. *Mean* them shits."

I hold my head down in defeat 'cause he's so right.

"I called our lawyer. He'll be here tomorrow. Tell that public defender it's a wrap for his ass. This gon' set me back, I know, but you my girl and that shit stand for something." I open my eyes wide.

"What you mean *I'm your girl*. Last week I was yo wife!"

"You know what I mean. It ain't like we married anyway, and you just address your own self as my girl, didn't you?"

A *Classy* THUG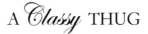

"Do you tell April that shit when you with her? Do you tell her I'm just your girl?"

"I'ma bounce 'cause you getting loud."

"THAT'S NOT GETTING LOUD THIS IS! WHEN WAS THE LAST TIME YOU BEEN WIT' HER? TELL ME THAT!"

"Hold it down over there," the officer yells out.

"See, you got them police in our convo. I know it's time for me ta holla at you another time. I put some money in the box out there, like 2G's. That should hold you. Call me and tell me what the lawyer said," he feeds me, rising up from the table, pushing his chair under it neatly.

"So that's it? We get like three hours for the visit," I mumble, feeling inadequate.

"You still sitting there. You gon' rise and kiss me or should I just get lost?"

I stand kiss him on his cheek and watch the only man I know how to love disappear right out the double doors. I scan the room, watching the ladies watch my man—the man I've been sharing with April since 10th grade.

Chapter 6
Zec

That woman she be doing wild shit. I just don't understand why she would even try ta take her brother coke, man. That shit ain't worth it. Coke get you more time than you made over time. I told her ta tell me when she wants something. I could've told one of my men to take that shit to him even though the fact remains I just took him money. I'll deal wit him at a lata date. Looking out for fam, now look at her—he can't do shit ta help. His ass ain't even ride out to see'a, I self talk on the the way to my sister's house.

I pull up in the driveway observing the surroundings, seeing if er'thing is er'thing. I have a funny feeling in my gut. I turn off my engine, step out my Denali, walk up the stairway. Sho nuff, it's only one of my killas posted at the front door. I jump out my Denali.

"Hey, Paul, where Johnny at?"

"He had a emergency at home, Sir."

"Emergency, huh?"

"Yes, Sir."

"Thanks," I tell him, turning my key to her front door, gaining entry.

Glancing at my watch I see it's 10 p.m. I move at snail pace through the house making sure all is ok. I look in my sister's room, she's not there. Moving to my daughter room, nothing. "Where could they be? she didn't tell me they was going anywhere."

I check out the basement, nothing. I go back up the stairs to the living room—

"Brandy! No, pleaz be alive please be alive!" I grip her body, yelling, "Where in the fuck is Nikki? Where is she? What happened?!"

"They got her ..." are her last words before she closes her eyes to meet her maker. I try franticly to give her CPR but nothing. I fall to my knees. "Why God?! Why you do this to me? I give to the poor. I do what I supposed to do for my family. This the thanks I get? Why?!" I cry out, feeling sorry for myself, my sister my child. I call all the men in the house.

"What Boss, wuss wrong?!" two of my killas ask.

Standing at my feet, "How did this happen? How did my sister die today? My daughter is gone! Who took my MOTHA FUCKEN CHILD WHO!" I yell, pulling back my sports jacket, brandishing my banga. They all look at one another, acting like Beavis and Butthead.

"Sir, I wasn't here. We just came on. We the second shift," one of them throws out there.

"The second shift crew you didn't see anything wrong like the fact Johnny not here. He gave you a lame ass excuse that his family was sick while my family in here dying. That's not what I pay you niggaz for. I pay you to make sure my family is safe!"

I call my main killa first. "Come, Dary."

He comes to me as ordered, moping along.

"Stand right her in front of me," I order.

He does what his told.

I grab him by his collar, pulling him closer. Using him as a shield I swing my heat around his back as I look over his shoulders.

Bloc, Bloc, Bloc! Killing the other three instantly.

I let my main man Dary go. Me and him been working together for 15 years; it was no way he did dis I'm sure of.

"What the fuck? Zec, you lost yo mind man!" he says, straightening his collar.

"Hell yeah my sister is dead! My child is gone, my wife in prison, somebody gotta pay!"

"I'm wit' you but damn man. I got balls to shit!"

"FUCK BALLS. WE GOTTA FIND MY DAUGHTER NOW NUCCA!" I tell him, breaking down, all the way down. Snot runs out my nose. He hugs me as I sob on his shoulder.

"C'mon man, stop crying. We gon' find the muthas that infiltrated and that's on my life we gon' find'em," he assures me.

I break our embrace, start stomping all over the floor like a marching soldier.

"THESE NIGGAZ WANT WAR, I'LL MAKE A FUCKEN WAR PATH FOR'EM!

Bloc, Bloc, Bloc! I put three more rounds in they asses 'cause I know it was one of'em, if not all of'me that played a fucken part!

Making my way to the door I look over at my sister, "Sorry sis, I can't give you a proper funeral. Dary, burn this shit," I order.

"On it, boss," he speaks back.

Chapter 7

Zec

"Somebody gotta pay for my loss. Why is my family getting caught in the crossfire?" I say to myself, parking my truck in front April's joint.

Letting myself in, all I can picture is my lovely sister's face before she took her last breath. *Who could it be and why?* are my thoughts, walking in the house.

"April," I call out.

"Hey baby, you came back to me early, huh bae," she runs up to me greeting with open arms.

"Some'em like dat. I'm not feeling too good. I just wanna lay down. I apologize."

"What's wrong, Dalla. What happened?"

"Inside shit. Nutten I can't handle. I'ma take a shower then get some sleep."

"Ok. You need me ta do anything?"

"I'm good."

"I didn't know you was coming. I would've made something to eat. Me and Barbie was going to the grill. I can stay if you want."

"Nah, you go ahead. I need some sleep," I tell her for the 10th time, it seems. "I came here 'cause I didn't wanna be alone. But you got plans. It's ok, though."

I go in her room, take my shit off, get a shower, dry off looking in the mirror at my face. All I see is Fury. I need answers. I need to holla at my mans James. That nigga told me he would be back tomorrow. For my sake, I hope he's back. This shit is getting harder by the minute. I don't even know where to start. Who even knew where my sister lived? Why would they take my daughter? Who was after my wife? What in the fuck is going on? My goons been wit' me all day, all night. So how they get past the ones I keep at my sister's? It gotta be an inside job. I got men here and April is safe. I don't get it. Nobody called for ransom for my daughter. I just don't get it.

I high tail it into April's room for some much needed rest.

She comes in with me.

"You still here? I thought you was going out."

"No, my man needs me. The grill gon' be there. I called Barbie and told her some'em came up."

"That's why I love you so much," I tell her, falling on the bed curling up under her breasts.

Chapter 8
Nikki

"Where am I? I'm so hungry and scared but I can't show it. Get me some food?" I yell through the dark room.

"Shut up in there. You eat when we feed yo spoiled ass."

"I'm hungry!" I yell.

The door I'm standing behind unlocks.

Whack!

A tear drops on the floor from my eyes. I look up at the man, holding the side of my face in pain. I've never been slapped before.

"Didn't I tell yo ass to shut the fuck up. Now get yo little ass back on that bed."

"But I'm hungry. Where is my daddy?" I protest.

"You not gon' be with yo daddy no mo. That shit is over."

"Stop talking to her like that. Man, she's a child," Uncle James walks up behind the mean man and says.

My eyes light up.

"Uncle James, you come to get me. Where is my daddy? Did you call him yet?"

"Here, eat this."

He hands me some McDonald's and a soda. I take it.

"How did you find me, Uncle James?" I ask.

"I didn't. These men gon' take you on a plane tomorrow. You just go with them. Your father gon' meet up with you where you going."

"Where is that? This don't seem right. That man said I'll never see my daddy again," I voice.

"I know, but your father is on board. You gon' be ok. That man don't know what he talkin' 'bout."

"Ok, but why you have me in this dark room?"

He looks at the mean man. "Take her in the other room so she can watch TV."

"Man, she's a brat. Fuck that, you take'a," he says, walking away.

"Come on, Nikki. He's just mean. He don't have kids," Uncle James explains. But something's not right. My gut is hurting. I know it's not right. I play along so I can stay alive for now. I'm doing all my daddy taught me.

Chapter 9

Errica

"I'm so happy the day is over for my ass. That shower was so hot, *whoo*. Now I'm gon' lay in this bed, finish reading this good ass book, then fall the hell ta sleep," I tell my celly.

"I know that's right. I saw you mowing the grass, girl. You be swinging that damn tractor, don't you?"

"I been swinging it for four years now."

"Errica, the red phone for you," this broad named Justice peeps in my cell to inform.

"For me? You sure? 'Cause it's another Errica in K6."

"No, they said Errica Hunter."

"Not today. I don't have time for this shit, not now. All I want ta do is get some much needed sleep," I tell my celly, who's curled up in the bottom bunk.

I mosey along to the center of the unit, where the phone sits on the horse shoe.

"Erica—51598-775," I spit my inmate number.

"Ms. Hunter, you have a visit."

I'm skeptical. "Are you sure? I wasn't expecting a visit."

"You are Erica Hunter 51598-775," she repeats.

"I'm on my way," I speak, hanging up the damn phone. I mosey my ass up to my cell.

"What was it? You not in trouble, are you?" my celly says.

"Nah, I got a visit. Not sure who it is. Whoever it is they betta be somebody I wanna see 'cause my ass is tired."

"I feel you on that," she says all curled up wit' a book.

I put on my full uniform, my tennis, then march over to the visit hall. The officer checks me in, opens the door to the hall. I stand and search the hall for somebody I know.

"E, over here."

"Chance, is that you?"

He waves me over.

"Hey you!" I exclaim.

"Hey yourself. You look good as always, even in here." He makes nice.

"Thanks." I smile, taking a seat.

"You want something from the machine?"

"Nah, I just ate."

"Well let me know if you do."

"Chance, what brings you here to see old me?"

"I was out of commission for a minute. Living in Sydney wit' my peeps. I came home like three months ago

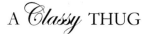

and shit. Last week I ran into my man Patrick. We was kicking it at the Penthouse. I asked about you. He told me you got popped. Concerned, I asked him where you was. He told me here, so here I am."

"But how you get in?"

"You tell me. I didn't know you had to be on a list until this man was talking about it."

"That's right. My cousin has a prior. I told him to be you. He filled out the app and got ID."

"That's fucked up."

"It' ain't like that. He cool. A good dude just got caught up wit' the wrong crew, that's all. He's in school doing good now. That was like six years ago when he got in some small trouble. So what you doing for a living? Smelling all good and looking like a million bucks."

"I got like three marijuana shops."

"So you a legit Good Fella now," I tease.

"You can say that. I see you still filling Earth wit' sloppy drama, huh?" he puts out there.

"Nah, not the Earth. Just general population, you feel that? I gotta do 20 years of it, so why not?"

I desperately wanna jump his bones about now. He looks so fucking good. He's brown skin, low cut hair, full facial trimmed hair close to his face, 6'3" wit' a shoe size 12 about 220 in weight and black eyes—*he is so freaking fine. My God I can't stand it.* We used to mess around until I met

Carton, one of the biggest dope boys in DC. Now I regret it 'cause I'm sitting in this muthafucka doing 20 years because of his bitch ass. The fucked up thing is he don't visit, don't come to see me, nor do he send money. His ass ain't shit.

"E, you know it's an unfortunate disservice to see you locked down in the cage. Who's your lawyer?"

"Public Defender."

"A what?! That nigga ain't get you a paid-for."

"No."

"What they lay you out on?" He's curious.

"Trafficking."

"Trafficking what?"

"Women," I lie. I can't tell him little girls. That lowlife had me doing shit for him I would never do.

"Whew. You know your lawyer's Ten?"

"Not off hand, but you can give me your Ten and email. I'll call you wit' it."

"You can email me?" He's lost.

"Boy, the FBOP done stepped up. I can skype you too."

"Dang, they did step up. They making all the money. Speaking of which, How can I send you money?"

"Through Western Union or Money Gram."

"How I do dat?" he asks, pulling out a tiny piece of paper.

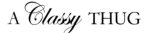

"You put in the state code. DC, the city code FBOP. Get a quick collect form Western Union, put my name and inmate number on it and there you have it."

"Got it. I'll do that when I leave this joint."

Me and Chance chop it up for three whole hours. It didn't seem like it though. He promises he'll come see me again and get me a paid lawyer. He's so nice, has always been such a classy ass thug. His ass always been a downlow God father. He know he'ing got no damn family living in Sydney. Now you know his black ass lying. He may have been in Sydney but not to see no fam for all them years. I believe he has a Marijuana shop, but it's a front fo' sho.

"I guess it's that time for us ta part. I see people getting up now," he makes notice.

"I guess. Chance, it's so refreshing to see your face. You really made my day."

"It's nice to make somebody's day," he tells me with a big smile, getting out his seat, leaning over putting his buffed arms around me. "Until tomorrow," he adds.

"You coming back here tomorrow?" I ask, all excited like a little kid.

"Yeah, I got a hotel. No need to drive 5 hours then don't stay."

"I hear that. So I'll prepare myself to see you tomorrow," I tell him, hugging him again just to smell that Creed cologne he's wearing. I can never forget that sent. That's one of the things I loved about him, besides that big ass 9 inch he's packin'.

Chapter 10
Zec

I hated to leave April so early this morning but I had to get on the road ta meet my man James, who finally hit me back. I turn onto the long driveway to our old private house ta take a shit; them turtles knocking for real. As I drive up I notice 3 trucks parked in front. I brush it off, thinking it might be some of my old frat brothers. Looking in my rearview mirror just ta make sho my killas in back, they damn sho are, both of 'em,

"Call Dan," I speak out to my auto phone.

"Dialing Dan."

"Yo man, what up?" Dan shoots.

"These cars I'm not sure of, so be on the lookout."

"Funny you mention that. We was wondering the same thing. We got you, dough."

To be sure I keep my engine going, check my hammer, making sure it's fully loaded. I step out my whip, head for the front door. The music is blasting. I peep through the old screen door. I can't believe my eyes. It's Bobby Mack from Andrew's crew. That makes a nigga concerned 'cause I know that nigga is grimey as fuck. Stepping back, I quickly leer at my folks, pull out my banga, they jump out they ride leaving they doors open, jogging towards the house. One heads for the back, Dan wit' me.

I wink my eye at Dan.

We walk up together, Dan in front.

Bang! Dan kicks the screen door in.

"What the fuck going on in here?!" I yell wit' our guns drawn.

One of the niggaz runs. Dan gives chase. The other has headphones covering his ears, playing games and shit with his back turned, sitting in the other room. My mans Meek creeps over to that nigga.

Bloc! Lights out for his ass.

We move strategically through the house.

Bloc! Bloc! Sounds like total black out for Bobby Mack as well. Meek musta peeled his wig back. I know the sound of that nigga's heat. Always two times, no more than three— that's how he rolls. So my heart is steady knowing it wasn't my man who got smoked. We continue moving through the house. We start opening closed doors.

"What the fuck?!" Meek whispers, turning to me.

I see many children, like five of 'em, gagged, tied down on an old dirty mattress. "Unloose 'em, man," I order Meek.

He places his one finger over his lips, telling the children, *Shhhh.* They nod yes. Dan gets right to it. I ain't never seen that nigga move so fast. He's untying them kids like he used to work on a fucken farm or some shit like that. I move out the room to another closed door. Nothing. Then another—

"WHAT THE FUCK?!" I yell, running to rescue my Nikki ... "Nikki!" I yell, sliding to my knees. I pull her up off the floor. Her body is so cold. "Meek, in here! Help, Meek!"

Dan runs up on me. "Shit, man. Nikki!" He pulls out his phone. "Man, we gotta call it in. We gotta get Nikki to the hospital man, we got to!"

"Put that dam phone down, nigga. We'll go ta prison!" I yell.

"Nah, you go take all the guns. We'll stay. We gotta get her to a real Doc, man we got to!" Meek walks up, stressing.

I know I gotta make a boss man's decision quick, or it's her life. I look at Dan. He nods, saying he's in.

"Give me y'all guns, man. I'ma leave her in y'all's hands. Save'a, man. Do what you gotta do." I take their guns, then vanish into the heat of the night.

Chapter 11

Errica

"Dada, my ass is so tired from this weekend. That nucca came the whole weekend. I can't lie, it did feel good to have a nice looking man come visit all weekend," I tell Dada, laying on my bunk. She takes a seat on the chair in my cell.

"Errica, so you think he really changed his life around. You don't need no shit in yours, not while you tryna do your appeal."

"He said fuck the appeal. He told me to fill out for a clemency."

"A what?! Why would you do that? I thought you had to have done half your time for that shit," she stresses.

"That's what I thought but he said it don't madda. He's like the fact is the nucca I'm covering for is out there doing him so why I gotta do all this time by myself. I ain't run shit. I was a stripper. Them girls wanted to sell they asses and they was 16 and 17. He was like, How about the ones on them streets that's 14 and 15? He said he got me. Whatever he meant by that, I don't care but the shit sound good," I tell my girl.

"You think he know somebody that can get you off in there?"

"Chance? Girl, I doubt it. His ass ain't big like that, at least I don't think. These days you never know who knows who, right?"

"What made you tell'em the truth? Yo ass said you wasn't gon' tell'em. Let me find out."

"He was like, E, come clean. Tell me everything. I can't help you if you don't. So I came clean."

"I hear you but my stomach says something ain't right. E, I'm far from jelly. A hoe want you ta go home but something's not adding up."

"Why you say that?"

"He popped up out of nowhere. Your cousin used to use his name to come see you. You said you told him all that and he was Gucci wit' it. That alone, a nigga ain't just gon' be a'ight wit' that shit. Then he say he gon' get you a lawyer, then comes and tells you to put in a clemency, he got you. Girl, sometimes you gotta use your own brain and know shit just don't add up. My man always said people do stuff for one reason—everyone is for themselves. Be careful, that's all I'm saying. Watch your back. Ain't nobody else gon' watch it, that's fo damn sho. Look at us now, being loyal to niggaz that don't give a fuck. We doing time for'em, so who's the real G's, you tell me," Dada states, crossing her legs, picking up a magazine off my desk.

"Dada, you spitting some real shit right there. I didn't look at it like dat. All I saw was I got a chance to get out this bitch. I promise I'll watch for all the signs," I tell'a with racing thoughts of my own.

"That's all I ask. I'ma get up outta here. Gots ta get some sleep. Sleep with the Angels, sis," she tells me.

"You too," I send back, still in deep, deep thought.

Chapter 12
Zec

"Man, I'ma hav'ta hit you later. Some shit just came up," I tell my man James over the waves.

"What man, you ok?" He sounds concerned.

"I'm good. I just have to get some shit done I forgot to do."

"Ok, I got some shit I was into anyway so it worked out for the best. Man, I'm still keeping my ear to the streets, tryna find out what happened wit' little Nikki."

I get silent. I want to tell him, but #3 rule: Never let your right hand know what you doing all the time; you never know who the culprit is for real.

"Thanks man, I appreciate that."

"Ok man, holla," he says.

"Holla, man."

After talking to James, I call my mans. My mind is focused on my little one. "Hey, man," Meek whispers.

"Everything's everything," I put out there.

"Man, I can't front. Them po-po up in this joint deep. The ET's got the kids. I'on know how this gon' play out. Nikki, she breathing. They took her in another ambulance. They questioning me and Dan but we got dat shit on lock. We coming down this way and shit to reminisce, then we saw some trucks out front, we stop in to see if it was one of Dan's old frat boys but shit ain't seem right, 'cause when he looked through the screen the niggaz had on wife beaters, chillin' … shit just ain't look right. So Dan kicked on the door and the nigga rushed us. Dan managed to grab one of the cat's guns. I grab the other niggaz gun, then I bust off. Dan said he grabbed the other nigga's gun. He ran and Dan gave chase. They seem to be ok wit' it for now 'cause we like heroes and shit. The brother cop said he thinks it will be all no charges 'cause they been looking for the kids for days. He also said he knows it's more to the story. Lots of holes, but he cracked a major case for them and shit."

"100,000 lawyer, no worries on that end, believe dat," I promise my mans.

"Man, I know you got us. We love you, man. She gon' be a'ight. They taking her to Children's hospital. The officer saying they gon' wrap it up here so we should be able to go soon. We got you."

"I know, man. I love y'all. I don't say it much but I do. That's why y'all niggaz still living." We laugh.

"I'ma wait until tomorrow, then I'ma go to the hospital," I tell Meeks. "Tell Dan thanks, man."

"Tell that nigga when you see'em, dough," he lets out.

"I got dis, man. Been doing this longer than yo young ass," I tell him.

"Fuck you, man," he jokes.

"One, man," I put out there.

"One, nigga," he repeats, then we end our call.

Chapter 13
Andrew

Me and my crew sit at the round table having a pow wow. I'm seated at the head of the table looking fresh as fuck, sporting my tailor made Jimmy Choo three piece fitted black & white suit with a pair of Valentino black & white dress shoes to match. Pushing my chair back, I take a stand. In a very steady clam voice, I start talking and walking around the table.

"Now I know something went wrong, something terrible went wrong, very wrong," I repeat.

"Ay, Boss?" one of my men seizes the moment.

Stopping him by putting an eye on his ass: "What's your name, son?" I voice.

"Alfonzo, Sir."

"Alfonzo, huh? What's your position, Alfonzo."

"A Street Sweeper."

"A Street Sweeper … Stand, son, when I'm addressing you."

"Ok, boss." Alfonzo stands. I peep he's kinda nervous though.

"My man, did you know your job is one of the most important jobs of them all?" I ask, giving Alfonzo a slight smile.

Alfonzo nods his head yes. I walks over to'em.

"Man to man, Alfonzo, you never fear another man. I don't care who that man is. I put my pants on like you do, one leg at a time. The only difference here son is that you wait until I ask you something, then you can speak." I smack him gently on his shoulder with my left hand as a sign of disrespect. It means he ain't shit ta me, sit yo wriggly ass down. Some of the seasoned men get it but not Alfonzo's rookie ass. His feet ain't wet enough yet. He looks uneasy as he takes his seat, happy I didn't off his ass for that shit.

"Back to what I was saying. We lost a lot of merchandise. Seven of them to be exact." I hawk eye James's ass. "Is there anyone"—I look at Alfonzo—"in here that can tell me how this loss came about? I mean a lot of time, merchandise, let us not forget the money, like two mill. How did it happen is my question?" I stop, brush off my suit. "Well, I'm waiting. Anyone know?" I look up, no hands up. "C'mon, it has to be somebody. Alfonzo, now is your time to vocalize."

A *Classy* THUG

Alfonzo says nothing.

"James, how about you?"

"No, Boss," James expresses.

"James, what do you know?" I add, shooting my eyeballs his way.

"I went to meet up wit' somebody, leaving Jr. and Mack. When I got back, cops was flooding that joint. I had no way in, Sir." James give his version of the story.

"When you got back? Wow, James, that's a strong statement being as though you're the ... let me see ..." I start counting on my fingers. "... Oh yeah, that's right, the *fourth* man in line of this here union, wouldn't you say James?" I positions myself behind James's chair.

"Yes, Sir," James speaks.

"Well, can you enlighten all your brothers as to how we all have taken a major cutback in our pay this month? A man such as myself got bills ta pay. Do any of you stand in my position?" I ask the others with my hands behind my back. All of them say yes.

James looks around the table. "Sir, as always your right. I abandoned my post. I have to pay the consequences, Sir. I'm lost as to what happened. I'm searching for the answer, Sir. I—"

I throw up my left hand. They all gasp under their breath, knowing what's next. I start moving around again.

"Good Fellas, I'm putting up a nomination that Mr. James Cutty goes in the hole for 30 days. Anyone else have a nomination?"

Alfonzo raises his hand.

"Mr. Alfonzo, you say?"

He stands. "Sir, I say 50 lashes."

"*Whoo*, that's a Street Sweeper. The killas of the union, 50 lashes on the table."

Another man raises his hand.

"Perry, you say?"

Perry stands. "I say 100 lashes."

"Thanks, Fellas. See, Alfonzo, this is how it's done. Good boy." Walking up to'em I place both my hands on Alfonzo's shoulders, signifying I'm not sure about him, but I'll let him live today. I sho nuff was gon' have him put in the inferno today. Alfonzo kinda knew that, I'm sure. "Ok brothers, write down your vote. 50 lashes, 100 lashes, or 30 days in the hole. James, takes heed. No one likes it when you're dipping in their pockets. I tried to let you off easy but they want blood. At least 30 days in the hole. You get 3 hots and a cot, plus a warm woman once a week. Your brothers don't seem to be feeling it, dough."

After they all vote, our Grand Master collects the papers, standing at the head of the table. Only the 1st high upper class 12 can vote, although I have 50 men at the table. The Master reads:

A *Classy* THUG

1. 50

2. 50

3. 50

4. 100

5. hole

6. hole

7. 100

8. 100

9. hole

10. 100

11. hole

12. 50

"We have four for 50 lashes, four for 100 lashes and four for the hole. Hear ye, hear ye, I the Grand Master of this union say we deliver 100 lashes to break the tie. All in agreement show with your hands." The Grand Master takes count and all agree.

But me, I say the hole. But it's out of my hands now—rules are rules. The Grand Master is always the tie breaker so it looks like 100 lashes. The Grand Master takes his seat.

"Damn, y'all ruthless. My apologies, James. Are you ready to walk the mile?" I ask.

"Sir, yes Sir," James says like a true soldier, no punk in his blood. He knows he messed up.

"Let us walk. Alfonzo, cuff'em. Big Black, bring the chains. I'm gon' pass the lashin' down to Alfonzo." I survey Alfonzo. "Can you do it, son?"

"I can. I sho can." He gladly smiles.

"It's *yes Sir,*" I correct him. "I see I'ma have'ta do a lot of work with you. Do you read, son."

"No Sir, I can't read. I only went to the third grade," he informs.

"The third grade, why son?"

"My mother told me I had'ta go to school, work or get out her house. I hated school, I hated her boyfriends so I got out. The streets raised me. Now I have a real home wit' you, Sir."

I hold my head down in shame. To think I was gon' smoke his ass. *I need to talk to my boss. We need to help our family more,* I think to myself as we walk the mile with James.

"Are you sure you can do this then?" I make sure.

"Yes, Sir," Alfonzo says with a slight smile. He hates James for some shit he did to'em last year, now it's payback time. I knew it, that's why I asked his 6'4" 260lb buff young ass.

Chapter 14
Zec

"Look at my baby, she gon' make it. She's gon make it. I know she is." I stand, press my head against the window of the ICU looking at little Nikki. She's helpless. The food them niggaz gave her had poison in it. Her tolerance level couldn't take it. I'm sure that's what it was. I'm just glad we got there when we did.

Andrew hedda not let me catch up wit his ass! I'm not feeling the fact that his crew into sex trafficking or whateva, but I'm gon' reach out and touch his ass fo' sho'. We supposed ta have a treaty. No blood shedding of family, crew, so what in the fuck happened? are my thoughts when the Doc walks up on me.

"Sir, she is fighting. She is doing better today than yesterday. We're doing a spinal tap to see if the drugs did any damage to her brain. Stay hopeful and pray."

"Thank you, Doc. I know you're working hard. Just work harder!" I tell his white ass, making my way out the door that reads exit.

I put in a call to April who was supposed ta meet me after going past the precinct ta see my wife.

"Hello," she greets, sounding all sexy.

"Hey you, how it go?" She brings a smile to my face.

"She doing fine. I don't think she was expecting me to come, though. Why you didn't tell'a I was coming up there?"

"I did tell'a. I told her last week I wasn't coming back up there. I told her you was gon' be coming up there ta take care of shit 'cause I had business. What, she acting funny or some'em?" I ask.

"No, she just seem kinda standoffish, that's all. I told her about Nikki; she didn't seem moved. I know she was hurting. She told me they was gon' move her to DC jail. She said she didn't know when though. She said she would call me when it happened. She told me to also tell you to stay out of trouble. She asked would you be at her hearings. I told her no. You said for me to step in, but like I said before I don't think she was feeling that shit, Zec."

"Is she not feeling it, or you not feeling it?"

"I was there, wasn't I?" she stresses with attitude.

"I told both of y'all we a family. When the shit get tough we all stick together. United we stand, divided we muthafuckin fall."

"I hear you. So when you coming back from out of town?"

"I'll be back when I get back. Just look after Nikki. If

they release her before I get back, I already put you down as my sister. I told them you would be up to look after her and take her home if need be. She knows you as auntie so that's dope."

"Zec, that goes without saying. You know I'm there on the real."

"That's one of the reasons I love you so much."

The line goes dead.

"April, you still there?"

"I'm here. I just never heard you say it before."

"Say what?" I'm baffled.

"The L word."

"Shawdy, you silly." I grin.

"No I'm real, and I love you too nucca. One."

"One, baby girl. One," I repeat, pressing the button to end the call, headed to Tampa, Florida.

Chapter 15
Zec
One Day Lata

I'm sitting at the beach wit' my man Tiny. We chopping shit up, enjoying the sunlight. Then I happen to look out into the beach; my eyes spot this chick, she fine as fuck! I mean super model fine as fuck!

"Dang man, who dat dough?" I let out strong as hell, still admiring her beauty.

"Where, man?" Tiny's blind old ass asks.

"Right there." I point, pulling on his right shoulder, positioning his body her way.

"*Whew we*, that right there youngin' is what I call money. Long ass money. But youngster, I think she outta yo league dough," he jokes, laughing.

"Oh shit, she's looking this way," I tell'em, looking up at the sky like a kid, fumbling my drink while tryna turn around in my chair ta face the bar.

Tiny's ass bust out laughing, ol' muthafucka. "Man, you actin' like you sixteen. She's just a lady. Go holla at'a if you want'a. She ain't no different than any other pussy," he continues to laugh.

"Man, I been out the meet and greet for like years. Women come to me, not me to them. What I say, man?"

"How about, Hello my name is ... What else?" Tiny schools me.

"You right, man. I'on know what I'm trippin' on, all the pussy I done had." I laugh it off on the real I got bubble guts.

I look her way. Our eyes lock, I do mean *lock* with mines. She's sitting on a beach towel beside another chick. *Man, she's so freakin' fine dough.* She's like a TV fine. Damn, her eyes, hell I think they like a color I neva seen before. They really dark, look like green, the greenest I ever seen in my lifetime. They like cat eyes, some shit like that. Her hair is blond and brown, laced down to her ass.

Ok, ok, she's standing, brushing the sand off her.

I bump Tiny with my elbow.

"I know, I see man, I see," he responds, drinking his beer.

Them calves so sexy and strong, her abs nice and flat, them arms nice, lil muscles just so. She got a black mole right above them sexy full pink lips, her titties like about 32C, that fuckin' waist rockin' 22 and them hips like 40. Now that ass

hittin' on about fake; well, I think it is 'cause it's too huge for her size. Dat joint is perfect round. *It's ok though, I'll take it, fake or not,* I tell myself, scanning her whole system.

I get up, walk her way wit' my drink in tow. Fuckin' sand getting all in my Valentino's and shit. I hope she's worth this shit for real.

"Hello, my name is Zec. May I ask yours?" I say, smiling from ear to fuckin' ear. She blushes.

"Hi Zec, who named you?" She's direct for sho.

"My grandmother. She named me after my uncle." *Dang, I'm tellin' her a lot.*

"Ok, named after your uncle. My name is Juswa."

"Wow, now that's a strong name you got dough." My ass still smiling.

"I like them golds. They kinda sexy. My mother named me after no one," she says gracefully with a big pearly white smile.

"Juswa, huh?" I say her name back to her.

"That's me, and if you can spell my name I'll let you take me out where ever you want." *She so fuckin' fine,* is all I can think.

Now I'm smiling, looking towards Tiny who's laughing his ass off. I put my attention back on her prettiness.

"If I can spell it? So you calling me stupid. We just met, Juswa. You gon' clown me like dat?" I joke.

"Well, can you spell it?" She stands, still glancing at me with them pearly whites and them deep ass dimples.

"Ok, let's make a deal. If I can spell your name I get to take you out for one week, and—"

She cuts me off. "There's an 'and'? Don't you think for spelling my name that'a be enough, you taking me out for a week?" she steps back stating her case wit' both hands on her soft-looking hips.

"Nah, I don't?" I tell'a, curling my top lip upward. That's the boss in me coming out. "We can't do more than dat," I offer. "I know you feel me, dough," I add, stepping getting up in her space.

She giggles. "So what is it?" she asks.

"What's what?" I'm lost right now.

"The other thing."

"Oh. You gotta cook me a meal, alone. Just you and me where ever you like."

"Now that I can do. That's after a week of you taken me out and paying for it no matter how much." She gets to the point, checking my wallet.

This chick must don't know. She can't think I'm a bum, I think to myself, standing in this hot ass sun.

"That'a work. Ok, here we go: It's J-U-S-W-A with a hyphen over the a. It's Italian, right? And it means *power*, right?" I cheese.

A *Classy* THUG

"Oh my God you like that man. I think you fit the silver slipper after the party the night before. You must be my prince. You're the first man that knew how to spell my name. How you know?"

A nigga cheesing hard right about now.

"How did you know? Really, tell me how?"

"On the real, no bullshit. I loved spelling in school. I wanted to be a teacher but I started my own business instead."

"Your own business? What kind of business is that?" She squints her eyes, holding her hand over them, protecting them from the blazing sun.

"I own real estate."

"You flip houses," she lets out like a black man such as myself can't own real estate.

"Nah, I have 12 real estate companies. Just for U Real Estate. You might heard of 'em."

"Who hasn't? They like all over the states and country. So that's how you knew my name was Italian. Your company is in Italy." She peeps my game.

"You got me."

We laugh.

Her friend walks up to us.

"Oh, I'm sorry this is my friend Penny. Penny, this Zec, the real estate man."

"Hi, Jasmine," I gladly greet.

"Hi," she says all sour, like she fuckin' ol' girl. She gotta be the ugliest ass butt fuck I eva laid eyes on. I don't know why ugly chicks always hanging wit' pretty broads. I don't get it.

"Look, here's my info," I tell'a, passing her my card.

Taking it, she gives me a grit.

"Some'em wrong?" I ask.

"Nope. I'm just wondering why you have on a suit on the beach in this hot ass sun, that's all?"

I take stock in myself, looking me up and down. Starting to walk away, looking back over my shoulder at her with a side grin, I say, "I thought all gentlemen dress in suits no madda where they go."

Hunching her shoulders, she says, "If you say so. When you taking me out?" she adds.

"How about tonight, to the Dolphins game?"

"That's in Miami though!" she yells.

"Don't madda. You let me worry 'bout dat," I tell her pretty ass.

"I gotta tell you I'm a Giants fan. They playing in New York tonight."

"New York it is. I'll pick you up at 12 noon."

"How about I get the tickets and pick you up at 12:00 noon?"

I snap my neck, twisting my whole body around. *This bitch is bad. She flipped dat shit on me. My kinda broad.*

A *Classy* THUG

I stop, asking, "From where?"

"Right here. I'll be standing under the hub," she states, pointing her long French manicured nail to the parking lot.

"Got you. 12 noon under the hub it is," I tell her, making my way through this hot ass sand wit' a drink that's probably watered down by now.

I get back to Tiny, who's engaged wit' a Power Ranger. *This bitch look like she'll beat my ass on any given day,* I think, taking my seat back at the bar laughing at my man Tiny. His ass take anything. He say he just love women.

Chapter 16
Zec

My driver pulls up to the hub at the beach in an all-black 1934 custom 4-door Ford Roadster. My driver stops the car right in front the lovely Juswa. He gets out, opens the back door where I'm sitting.

Beaming, she states, "This how you doing it?" She steps in the back with me. "We sure are going to the airport in style, ain't we?"

"It's no other way to travel," I utter.

We ride the way to the airport. I get to know her more. She seems to be really cool for such a fine ass lady. She's six years older than me. No children. She came to this country with her father. He's Italian, living in the NY. Her mother was killed when she was ten in Canada. She loves to eat seafood, loves old music, dance, plays chess and get this—she loves to play B-ball. That shit made me raise a brow. Can't wait to play'a. All in all she seems to be so honest and pure.

I've neva met a girl like'a. We pull up to the private terminal. The driver lets us out.

"Have a good trip, Mr. Smith."

"I'm sure I will," I tell'em with a wink.

"We're going private, is dat ok wit' you?"

"I mean you got the tickets, I could at least provide the ride."

"I get it but you must know I'm a real woman. Real women can hold their own, feel me?"

"No I don't and never will." I short sight her ass with a serious face. "Boo boo, we not gon' do the 'I'm a woman, I got my own bullshit', right?"

A smile lights up her face. "We going private on you, huh?" She inspects the outside of the jet.

Now I smile. "That's the only way ta go," I tell'a as we board the jet.

Taking our seats, we start talking and laughing more and more. The jet engines start. Minutes later we take flight.

The jet is quiet. I check to see if Juswa is sleep. Our eyes gaze into one another's. My fucking heart jumps. Now dat shit right there some new shit for a nigga. She has this glow about her I didn't notice at the beach earlier.

She speaks, "You make me laugh when I want to cry. Make me live for the moment when the news I just found out makes me want to die. You make me smile when I want to frown. You're making me believe in me again when I

know no one else really does, Zec. This right now is what I call happiness." Her eyes turn a darker green, her smile fades, she crosses her legs, resting her arm on the arm rest of the chair. I'm thinking how a street nigga like me gon' top that shit. Maybe Tiny's ass was right. Maybe she is out of my league. Guess I need to find some serious shit ta come back wit' quick.

"I'm happy as well. It feels good to know I can make you feel all those things. You only live once. Why not lift off with me," I whisper what I call love nothings to her while lifting out my seat taking a seat beside her. I wrap my arms around her. She gives me the look of approval, lays her head on my shoulder.

"Zec?"

"Yeah, boo."

"Thanks, but that was weak as fuck. The thing is you tried and that's what matters to me. So thanks."

"You're welcome." I close my eyes for some much needed rest, thinking of her but also not forgetting my daughter that's fighting for her life back home.

Chapter 17
Deja

"All rise for the Honorable Judge Morris."

"I can't believe Zec's ass ain't have nobody contact me. His ass wrong. He gon' do me like this. What's he doing?" I ask myself as I stand before this judge.

Glancing behind me—nobody, not even his hoe April. I still can't believe he be sending her up here to check on me. What a dog. *I got something for they asses when I touch down. I don't even know how my child is holding up. I feel so damn helpless,* I continue to think, holding back my tears.

"You all may be seated," the Judge orders.

"Attorney Henry. I see we're making this quick. Your client has entered a plea of guilty."

"Yes, Sir, as you already know we went over it two weeks ago. She would like to be sentenced today, Your Honor."

"Ms. Colman, do you have anything you would like to say to the court before I sentence you?" the Judge appeals to me.

"Your Honor, I have a child who is fighting for her life. She needs me. I understand what I did was stupid. I was reckless from the start. The man who put the drugs in my car, his name is Kurt McKing. He's dead now," I blurt. *Sorry, Kurt, my child needs me,* I say to myself, not really feeling like a rat 'cause he's dead so it don't madda. At least that's how I feel.

The judge raises his head, looks at the prosecutor then my attorney, not expecting me to say what I just said. The judge calls them both to his bench.

In about 5 minutes they both return to their seats. The judge speaks up. The prosecutor looks my way.

"Are you willing to give information on one Kurt McKing's operation?"

"Sure," I answer.

My lawyer nods at the prosecutor who hard looks at the judge.

"Ms. Colman, I'm proud of you. I will sentence you to 67 months and suspend 37, which will give you 37 when you go to Federal prison. You will get 18 more months off for the drug program I'm recommending. I do hope you learn something while you're in there. Your rule 35 will go into effect as of today." He hits his gavel. Court is adjourned.

I could do the time but my daughter is more important so I'll give up Kurt's people, not mines or Zec's. They some small out of town New Yorkers anyway. *Who cares, they'll never know,* I think to myself, mugging my lawyer I smile from ear to ear ... *I'm not gon' ever tell Zec when I'm coming home or what I did. Just gon' lace my boots up, meeting him and April ass on the flip side.*

Chapter 18
April

This can't be happening. Zec ass ain't answering his phone. He been gone for a month and he hasn't answered his phone for a whole week. That shit is out of the question. *What's going on wit' his ass? I know he said he was going to be off the grid, but really?* I ask myself as I look at my bank account that reads $3,000. I used all the money in the other account sending his fucking wife money, maintaining my life and his daughter's. He has to realize I'on have money. He gotta know it takes money for his child. *I damn sho know he don't think I'm going in my funds for his wife*, I think to myself.

I try calling him one more time before bed. Right to voicemail, needless to say the fucker is full. That means he's not even checking it. Oh no, a thought just came to me: "I hope he's ok!" I say out loud while seated at the computer. Let me try texting him for the one hundredth time.

April: Zec I hope u ok miss you call or text low on funds child needs father and funds.

Zec: I'm on my way to the bank I told Nikki to tell you she musta forgot.

April: U talking to her but not me?

Zec: Chill I'll be home next week busy.

April: What eva ok.

"I'on know what's going on. I'm so happy his woman got 37 months though. I'll have him all to myself. Me, Nikki, it's about time," I say out loud before sending him my last text.

April: Luv you miss you.

Zec: I hear that. Busy gotta go ...

No he didn't end it like that. One month I'm taking care of his child, taking her to her doctor's appointment and this is the pay I get? Ok, April, he might just be doing some real business tryna make stuff work out for our benefit.

Chapter 19
Chance

Wit' my assassins squad at bay, I thought I'd do a little shopping for my mother. I put her in a resting home as soon as she started talking out her head. I was at her house three months ago when she asked me to get her teeth off the dresser. Number one, when she start laying her teeth around like that in no container? Number two, she don't have no food in front her so why she need her teeth? I was like, "Ma dukes, you not eaten. Why you need your teeth?" She was like, "Boy, I got a date tonight. You need to mind your business."

I laughed so hard at the same time I started thinking it's time. She's 80. She needs some kinda help. I sho can't be here all the time for her. My older sister was mad at me. Nevertheless she lives in West bum fuck so who gon' be responsible for Ma dukes. Not her.

After I'm done shopping I reroute myself towards the food court. On my way I peep that nigga Zec headed down my path. I'on like the look on shorty's face. I eye my squad, putting they asses on alert, not sure if he's coming to commission or partition I wrap my hand around my bitch, pulling her ass waist high, waiting fo' dis nigga ta flinch. One wrong move I'ma blast his ass to hell. Now Zec knows my power-gate so I doubt he's gon' try shit today.

He stops dead in my track.

"Wussup," he shoots.

"Wussup yo," I voice, keeping my bitch on standby, not discounting his killa blood, the same blood I bleed.

"That nigga Andrew," he swiftly lays on me.

Lowering my baby I take time to listen. "What's up wit'em?" I ask, keeping a watchful eye. Seeing as though he's rolling one shot, I eye my niggaz, let'em know ain't shit happening today.

"Dat nigga kidnapped my daughter."

"Kidnap yo daughter? That's a heavy bone ta lay down on somebody," I tell'em.

"Not really, knowing y'all get down," he spits venom.

I hesitate to speak on it 'cause I haven't talk to my commander.

"So say. I ain't holla at'em lately, you know. Seems you know more than meets the eye."

A *Classy* THUG

Skepticism alludes his eyes. I pretend not to care, making sure my fine baby soft face stay on relax mode, feel me.

Flicking his thumb off the side of his nose, he takes his stand. "Let me get dis, you saying you got yo clique picking up tar for a black top but you'on know what product they buying wit yo green heads. Shit sound like some imperial not superior." He fronts dat shit to me like I'ing standing here bossed the fuck up.

"So Zec, we raising cattle now or this some old misunderstanding?" I stand in front him full-fledged for whateva.

"Chance, I don't make it a habit to beef wit impotent muthafuckas. You clammed up like a bitch when I approached. I see yo slay bitch ass niggaz that's how weak yo game is. I tell you what, if my daughter dies today you gon' eat that muthafuckin cattle."

My eye jumps. I wanna handle his bitch ass right here in the middle of this mall. I can't let my emotions get the best of me. Not today, too many cameras. I lean in just so making sure he hears me.

"I disembowel bitch niggaz like you so consider yourself one. Conversation over." He steps back with a big ass grin on his face, twinkles in his eyes.

"Cash dat shit, nigga," he voices.

I smile, starting on my way, not knowing what the fuck just happened, who his daughter is, why didn't Andrew inform me about the shit. Is Zec right? Have them niggaz been selling product behind my back? Now I got a beef wit' one of the most notorious executors in Washington, DC. I'ma have'ta pay my commander an informal visit. My day was going good. Always some bullshit in this fucked up game.

Chapter 20

Chance

I'm in Andrew's driveway, not knowing what to expect. I park, make it around the back of his house. Peeping through his basement window I see two under-ages tied to a pole. Leads me to think, product for sho. Pulling on his door knob, it's locked. I reach over the door, feeling for the key. *Ah, got it.* Opening the door, I follow the moaning sounds. I feel my heart beating rapidly. I enter the room.

"OH SHIT!" I yell.

Andrew jumps up butter ball naked, glancing in my direction. "Man, give me a minute."

Expeditiously, I apologize. Falling backward, I go to the sitting room pouring me a much needed strong one, taking a seat.

"Sorry you found out like this," he voices, coming out the room.

"Not as sorry as me." Avoiding the subject.

"You wanna talk about it, man?" he fishes to see where my mind is at this point. After seeing that nasty shit, my words evade me. I forgot what I came over for. My mind is blown.

"Nah, I'm good. Shit, you made me forget why I came. Shit, oh yeah. What's up wit' Zec's daughter?"

"Huh?" He looks baffled.

"Yeah he stakes claim you kidnapped his daughter." I put it out there.

"Nah, that shit was James. He got 100 lashes for it too," he tells me.

"100 lashes? Man, that's it. Y'all know better. We got an alliance wit' Zec's clique. Ain't James Zec's boy and shit." I need some clarity on shit.

"Right, but—"

I cut his ass off. "Ain't no buts. Er' thing behind *but* is bullshit, so tell me the hearsay—who authorized the snatch?"

"James took his daughter just because. I guess on some ol' Cain and Able shit, who knows. The thing is Zec got'a back and James suffered the penalty," he tells me like it's ok. Like a baby got her bottle and she stop crying. *Shit.*

"That's not it. While you slipping, I gotta hold back the lighting behind all dat shit. See, I ran into Mr. Zec himself today blindsided. He didn't seem happy about none that shit. I gotta put out a fire that I didn't partake in. That nigga

want a war. One he got all rights to wanting too," I tell this sheep-fucking muthafucka.

"I say we give his ass what he want. Who is he? Ain't nobody scared of his ass," he tells me. "What we just gon' punk out?" he adds.

I look at his stupid ass. "Why would I lose soldiers over one good for nutten fuck? You tell me."

"I see your point."

"Do whatever it takes to make this shit right. Now I'ma let you get back to fuckin yo sheep." I look at'em in his black robe. My stomach still churning from the sight of dat nigga fuckin a live sheep. All I can see is that sheep duct taped around its mouth and his dick up in it. That shit is crazy, ain't never seen no shit like it before in my entire life—and I seen some shit … Damn, fucking a sheep from behind like that shit is normal. He needs help for real. All the pussy be coming at his ass, he picked an animal. *What the fuck is happening to this generation these days?* I ask myself walking towards the door.

"Oh before I forget. When you shipping the product out?" I regretfully ask since we lost so much this week.

"Tomorrow morning."

"The ones I saw tied to your pole in that room, they product too?"

"Yes."

"From now on I want you to call me. Give me the number er' week on product, feel me? I'ma be putting in a camera as well in each station. Get them out tonight," I give a direct order.

"You the man," he runs back.

"For sho." I raise two fingers. Deuces. *A fuckin sheep ... what is the world coming too,* I think to myself.

Chapter 21

Zec

After my little tongue boxing match with Chance, I pull up to my pretty girl Juswa's house in VA. Inspecting her driveway, it seems she has company. Raising my phone to my ear I call making sure my inner wishing is correct.

She picks up. "Hello?"

"Hey, what you doing?' I surely ask.

"Nothing, waiting on you," she makes known.

"You sure about that?"

"What, why you ask that?"

"I'm out front, that's why."

"Oh my. New Phantom Rolls-Royce?" she asks with excitement.

"She's nice. Come open the door."

"Ok, but we gotta get you a key," she starts, standing in the doorway wit' some come-fuck-me-shit on.

I park my shit behind hers, walk up to her, taking her soft lips in my mouth.

Breaking our kiss, she says, "Why you just getting here?"

"If I knew it was gon' be like this I would've been here. Had some light shit to take care of, nothing big at all."

She starts laughing, running up the steps. I give chase.

Not being able to see her fine ass: "Where you go?" My guess she's playing hide and seek.

"Get undressed. Lay on the bed," she yells from somewhere close. I take my shit off, place my peacemaker under the pillow. I can't be too sure. I can't neva trust nobody, not even the bitch I'm fucking. I lay on the bed and wait.

"*Zeeec*," she calls my name all sexy. I sit up.

Now that's what I call beautiful.

Turning the lights out, Juswa stands in the doorway holding a lighted white glass candle. I rub my eyes, making sure they not fuckin deceiving me. Noticing her shapely body I get up, moving closer to my queen. Standing in front her my hands tighten around her tiny fragile waist.

"I want to be the dominant one tonight," she whispers, giggling, still holding on to the candle that's reflecting her beauty.

I bring my soft finger to her lips.

Shh my lips motion. "You could never be dominant. I'm always gon' be your man, the man," I assure her.

A *Classy* THUG

Removing the burning candle from her hand, I sit it on the table that's positioned beside us. Moving closer, she feels my manhood rearing up I know. My eyes grow wicked hot. My breathing is heavy as a mu-fuck. Her hands take a stroll down my bare chest. Picking her up, our eyes dissolve into one another's. I lower her into the soft white sheets. Pressing my body on top of hers, kissing her deeply, grinding my tongue against hers. Hot blood flows through my body to my brain; this shit I never felt in life. I suck her in my world, taking her ass to heaven wit' me no doubt.

I pause, as much needed breath escapes my throat, seeing her eyes half-closed, her lips still parted with excitement. I reach between her soft thighs, touching her intimately, pressing down on her clit with slow deliberate strokes with my fingertip. She arches her back, lifting off the sheets, slightly indicating she wants more.

"You like that?" I whisper.

"Ummm," she moans, nodding a response of yes.

"Say you want more," I demand.

"I want more," she moans in waiting.

I lower my head to the full mound of her lovely breast. She breaths deep, whimpers from her small parted lips. I slide two of my long, thick fingers inside her raspberry pie, taking her peaking nipple inside my mouth, sucking gently. She moans my name.

"Zec, Zec, oh pleaz, make love to me."

Her curves undulate beneath me. She's so incredibly soft, so warm, I cling tight as my penis demands attention, guiding its head to her inner worth. She hisses.

"Um oh um shit."

We evaporate together in licentious heat until we become liquid. Juswa's body is hot like she's building a climax. Sweat breaks across my back, pressing harder, sliding along a path of love. I can't seem to get enough. I nut over and over, hoping she's feeling the worth that's exploding within her nest.

Rising up: "Zec, I ... I ... I Love you so much."

My ego is happy to hear those words. Shifting gears, I thrust harder, deeper than ever.

"Zec, Z! Oh my God, Zec!" she screams, digging her long polished nails in my back. She draws blood.

Pulling my dick out, I explode all over her upper body. She lays back as my tongue lightly brushes against her pink clit. Moving her hips, she continues calling my name faster. My tongue rotates. She digs into the bed, swerving like a snake, arching her back higher.

"Zeeeeeec," she lets out, her body trembling in silence.

Laying my body on her, I take her into my arms, kissing her passionately as I guide my dick back in her garden of Eve. *She just don't know how bad I need her tonight,* I think as I pump all my emotional stress into her love nest.

Chapter 22

April

The next day after me and Juswa's love session.

Standing in my living room waiting for Zec's ass is making me more frustrated by the minute. That nigga said he'll be here at 12 noon; it's five. On top of that his ass ain't answering his cell. I'm 'bout sick of 'em. I was talking to my mother last night. She was like, "Maybe if you tell him about your secret—"

I cut her ass off. I was like, "Hell no. Knowing his ass, he'll kill me." I gotta get my money up somehow. My ass is addicted to shopping too much. I pick up the phone, trying again.

"Hello?"

About time, my mind wonders.

"Zec, where—?"

He cuts me off. "Don't start. I'm on the beltway—"

I cut him off. "That's what you said 12—"

He cuts me off. "I know what the fuck I said 'cause I was the one who said it, *damn.*"

I start going on his ass. All of a sudden I hear a beep. Taking the phone from my ear with one hand on my hip, "I know my line didn't just go fuckin dead. Did that bastard just hang up on me?!" I yell.

My impulse says call back, get in his shit. My psyche says otherwise.

Putting on a pot of coffee, my mood springs from left to right.

"Fuck his ass. He not gon' be treating me like I'm pedigree," I self talk, pouring my coffee in my cup.

Sitting down taking a sip, giving Zec all my head space—his dick ok, his head off the chain, money fair, attitude sucks. My fine soft baby. I'm thinking I can do better, just too lazy to try. I'm sitting here looking out for his wifey and child. His daughter is over his Aunts—that's where she's gon' stay. As for sending money, taking messages to his fucken uppity wife—find another mule; this hoe is done.

"I'm here now. What's that shit you was talking earlier?" he grabs my face wit' one hand.

"What I say?"

The compression of his hand feels like a fuckin vise grip. All of a sudden I feel my ass elevate from the chair like I'm levitating. This nigga swings my body across the fuckin floor. Coffee flies everywhere. I hit the floor sliding.

A *Classy* THUG

My back crashes into the wall. Taking hold of my neck, he jerks me up by my throat, squeezing it.

"April, I got too much shit going on. All you do is complain!" He squeezes tighter. I'm losing air. I kick harder but my kick lands on his steel stomach. He throws me on the couch. I feel like I'm on a gotdamn roller coaster. Ripping my dress in two, he yanks my thong to the side, spitting on my pussy lips, his shit fully erected, lays between my soft legs, sticking his dick in, riding me like I'm a rag doll. I can't believe it. The one-minute nigga is fucking for an hour and he's cumming back to back.

Where is he getting this stamina from? I start thinking about someone else so I can stay wet, 'cause I'm hating him about now.

In about an hour and a half of watching the clock, he releases me, raises, grabs his shit, vanishes into my bedroom. I ball up in a knot, not believing this. Asking myself what's wrong wit' his ass. I've never seen him act this way. I wonder, *Do he know my secret?* He comes back to the living room.

"Why you still laying there? Who been in here, huh? Who?!" he yells, spit flying everywhere.

I look up at'em.

"What you talkin about? No, nobody been in here but you! What in the fuck is up wit' you, Zec!"

"How these tighty whites in here? Tell me that? I'ing be wit' nobody else but you!" He holds up some Fruit of the Looms briefs.

I'm busted. What can I say? So I hit him with the guilt trip.

"Why you care? You don't answer your phone. You used me up. You don't wanna be with me. You got a wife, nigga. Hell, you trained me to take care of'a when you out banging other hoes!" I get up the nerve to say. How I get the nerve up, I'll never know.

"What you say, bitch? What you say?!" He moves in closer. "I trained you, bitch. I take care of yo ass, I pay the fuckin mortgage on this bitch! It's me that pay yo bills. You gon' sit here and tell me you got another fuckin hard ass coming up in here in my shit!"

"Whatever!" I stand in front him, my arms across my chest, patting my foot wit' my lip curled. My back hurting like a mug, though. After what he just did to me, I'on know what I'm thinking. I guess I'm just tired of all his shenanigans.

"Whatever? What *ever?!* That's all yo ass gotta say?!"

"Zec, fuck you!" I finally tell his black ass, walking towards the bedroom.

"Fuck me? Fuck me? No, bitch, fuck you!"

Click-clack was the last sounds I would here for life.

Chapter 23
Zec
The next day

Damn, I didn't mean to kill'a ass. Shit. I called my mans to come clean her house up, instructing them to dump her body anywhere. Shit, my nut all in'a. Fuck, what was I thinking? They gon' have'ta chop her body up, then burn it. What in the entire fuck was going through my mind? I'm stressed. That broad ain't do shit to deserve that shit. She just couldn't keep her mouth shut. She knows my get down. I don't understand why she put me to the test of no return. *How I'ma face her mother? How?* I think to myself, turning the corner to the prison.

I need to see this dumb ass snitching bitch. I told her to lay low. I was gon' take care of her ass. I told her to go ahead, take the plea, I'ma have you out of there soon. But nahhh ... she had'ta turn on my boy. He's dead, may he rest in peace, but still she know how this shit go. She didn't hold up to the street code. She got diarrhea of the mouth. She just don't get it. She told on his connect, which is my connect as well. They know she did that cross-training shit too. She should know by now they got inside men. Don't she know that? Now I gotta go take care of this shit. Man, she so fuckin dumb. I'm not losing my connect for her ass, hell no. I think hard and long to myself.

Parking my shit, I get out. Open the door to the prison. Man I hate the smell of prison, more less coming ta visit. Fuck, had she listened to me she wouldn't be here.

I check in and wait for her ass to come out. As I wait I notice Chance ass, wondering who he coming to see. I guess I'll find out in a minute. Looking at the vending machine, I go get some shit I think she'll like. I love Deja; she's my ride or die. She's just not Juswa. Maybe a nigga is moving too fast. They say the grass always looks greener on the other side. Juswa, she's so damn fine, so intelligent, sweet, soft. She's not 'hood, she's normal. I like that. Maybe she's just something different or the real tall drink I need.

I get the stuff, head back to my seat. I feel Chance looking at me so I shoot his ass a mug shot, reminding him shit ain't sweet between me and him. This nigga mugs me back. It's ok, though. One thing about that nigga he know I make niggaz pay what I weigh. All 2 pounds of it, adding one more pound with my finger around the trigga.

Chapter 24
Errica

Boredom got me standing outside my cell leaning against the top rails of my unit, checking out the new Fish. One of 'em look kinda like this broad I knew from high school. Her name was Deja Queen. Needless to say when I scanned the in-bound sheets this morning her name didn't appear so my eyes must be deceiving me. Shifting my conversation back to Dada, I see Train peddling her feet across the unit to greet'a. I went to school wit' Train, too.

"Dada, that girl right there." I point. "Do you know her?" I ask.

"She look like that uppity bitch from when we was in Suitland high. Her name some shit like Dege or Dejo, some shit like that. She wasn't in my circle so I can't remember her name," she feeds me.

"Deja? Was it Deja Queen?" I ask.

Snapping her fingers, "Yeah, that's it. Deja, that's it."

"But I checked the roster out this morning. Her name wasn't on it," I inform her, still checking Deja out.

"Maybe they didn't put'a on it. Maybe she's under another name. You know how the FED's do."

"Maybe," I say, thinking she's Zec's wife, why would she be in here? I didn't hear nothin' 'bout no 'hood niggas going south. I gotta know. I flip flop my shower shoes down the steps to the lower tier, right up to'a.

"Deja?" I call out, smiling all phony like the rest these bitches.

"Yeah," she answers like she'on remember that fight we had in 9th grade. I smashed that ass.

"It is you. I thought it was. Wasn't sure though, let me help you," I offer.

"I got it," she claps onto her roll, hightailing it to her cell. Her roll is her blankets, sheets, shit like that.

"Deja, I know you used to doing stuff on your own but baby this world ain't like dat. You need friends in here," I school.

Stopping at her cell door, she turns, meeting me face to face.

"I know. I just left county. Real talk, Errica, I know how you play cards. I'on get down like dat. I don't respect nobody that gets down like dat."

"So I'm being judged when you don't know the whole story? I know you not going off street gossip."

A *Classy* THUG

Dropping her roll, "I'm ears." She grew balls over the years. I'll give'a that much.

"The girl was 17 years old. That part is right but they said they was 18-19-20. Some said 21. I didn't know, ok? I've been judged doing time for my no good ass man. Now I'm here. 20 years in front of me. Can you feel that shit?"

"What man, Errica? Timber?" Sarcastically, she curves her lips, putting that shit out there.

"Hell no, girl, left that dried up California prune after high school." We laugh.

"My bad, Ma. I'm just in a mood, that's all. Pushing off some other, feeling sorry."

I can imagine. I remember lacing my pussy all over her man just before I got locked down. So I know she going through it. *I'ma trick his $1,500-minute dick ass again when I get out this peace,* I think to myself,

"It's all good. I remember when I first got popped. So what you in for?" I'm being nosy.

Her eyes water. "Coke. Some small shit. I'll be home soon. So who's your man now?" She changes the subject. I guess it's too touchy.

"Andrew," I say.

Frowning her grill, "You fuckin wit' grimey ass Andrew?"

"I used to. Yes, he's grimey. Left my stupid ass in here dangling. That's how it goes when you true to the code. He out there doing God knows what." I give it to'a raw.

"So when you going home?" Now she's being nosy.

"Who knows? Chance working on something for me."

Placing her hands on her imagination, "You mean fine classy clean cut pretty boy Chance Mayweather? I'ing seen his ass since Jesus was a baby." We laugh again.

"You right. He just popped up outta nowhere. He's always been a goodhearted dude. He stays to himself, neva knew his work. He's a walk alone type gangsta," I inform.

"Ain't that the truth," she voices, now making her bunk up.

"At least you on the bottom." I make small talk.

"They can have this shit. I'd trade you the bottom for home and time. You just let me know."

We laugh, then talk about old times until I hear my name over the loud speaker to report to the visit hall.

"Well, that's my Chance."

She laughs.

"I gotta go," I say. "I'll hit you back tonight. Maybe we can watch some good movies. It's movie night. The listings is on the board. I'll tell Dada to come see you."

"Dada from school?"

"Yep, her square ass is here. But she not square no more. Honey, she grew her ass up."

"This I gotta see. You enjoy your vis—" Before she could get the word visit out, they called her name over the speaker as well for a visit.

A *Classy* THUG

"I wonder who that could be?" She looks puzzled.

"Might be Zec," I tell her.

"Might be. Well, I guess we can walk together."

"Let's move like in 5 minutes," I voice.

"See you in five."

Chapter 25

Errica

My day lights up seeing Chance waiting for me in the visiting room in his usual seat.

"You a'ight?" Chance flashes a small smile.

"I'm as good as can be … considering," I express, taking a seat.

"I got good news," he says.

"You do?" My ears perk up.

"My lawyer said you should be outta dodge in a week or so."

I bend all the way into the table. He's positioned across from me.

"You lying. Don't be lying to me," I whisper.

"Have you eva known me ta put my words on front street wit' out backin'em up?"

"Neva!" I get happy as hell.

"Start packing, E," he laughs.

I jump up, yelling, hollering. I can't believe it. I wanted to run over to Deja but she looks so sad. Chile, please, I can't let nothin' ruin my mood.

"Mrs. Hunter, quiet down over there," one of the officers says.

My ass obliges, not wanting shit to hold me in here.

"Slow down, Ma. You bringin' all eyes this way," he tells me.

"I'm just excited, sorry," I say, taking my seat after giving his ass a big hug.

"No need to apologize. You on that celebrate time."

I calm my happy ass down quickly.

"What's been happening in here?" He asks me this but his eyes wander. Following them, I land on Deja.

"You remember her?" I ask, still looking her way.

I guess I broke his trance from school.

"Deja, the girl you focused on right about now."

"You got me."

"Do you know her was my entire question?" I repeat.

"Yeah. What she in here for?" He's being nosy.

"Powder. On a run for some man, her car flipped. Them loads fell out. Here she lies."

"That's fucked up. I need you to do me a favor." He lays it out.

"Boy, anything. What?" Hell, if he ask me to fuck her for him, I would. His ass getting me a get out of jail free card.

"Relay this message for me, just like this." He tells me the message. Don't know why he thinks she don't know, but I'll play his little game.

"You want me to do it now?"

He gives me the look.

I go over to her, ask her to come to the bathroom for a minute. After speaking to her fine man, she walks with me. I regretfully start giving her the message.

I return back to Chance once I'm done playing inspector gadget.

"It's done," I let him know.

"Good, baby girl I can't wait to you get the fuck outta here what you gon do when you touch down to get money?"

"I'm going back to Ebony Inn where eva to get my hand wet, feel me."

"I do."

We continue to talk about old and new days. All I can think about is getting outta here so I can get back at Andrew's ass.

Chapter 26
Deja

I'm visiting with Zec, surprised he came to see me. I see Errica visiting with Chance. I get kinda envious. He is so nice, so fine, such a man of men.

"So how is things going out there? Why didn't you bring our daughter?" I ask.

"I wanted to come by myself. Look, why you rat on Kurt's connect?"

"I didn't. I just gave them Kurt. How would I know his connect?" I lie.

"So you know when you ratted him out you stepped on my toes. My man called me for a meeting, telling me you ratted him out. You know he got a mole, right? You do know this? You tryna save yourself when I told you to stay in the paint, I was gon' straighten you out. What happened wit' you not takin' my word for platinum no more?"

"It's not that. It was Nikki. I couldn't stand not being with her. Z, all that poor girl has is me and your sister to love on her."

"Deja this me, though." He points to his chest. "I told you one thing, you did another. Now what I'm supposed ta do?"

"Zec, what you saying? You gon' put a hit out on your own wife, the mother of your child?"

"I told you not to do something, so what's the consequence behind it supposed to be?"

I take a deep breath. "Zec, you taught me well. I'm not afraid of death. I seen to many bitches/niggaz get splayed by your hands, mines, so what you saying, give it to me straight?" Now I'm relaxed, remembering they make pine boxes for his ass too.

"They coming for you. Ain't shit I can do. You gotta take your testimony back, D. You gotta, or them NY white cats coming. Why you put—?"

Errica comes to the table, interrupting us.

"Excuse me. Hey, Zec," she says to him like they fuckin'. Knowing his ass they was at one time or another. "Look, Deja, I gotta tell you something that happened in the unit. It kinda involves you."

"Oh, ok. What is it?"

"It's kinda private. I mean you can tell him if you like after I tell you. Can you walk wit' me to the vending machine?"

"Ok I'll be back, Z."

Following her, we stop at the soda machine. "I don't know if this is true. I don't make it a habit to get into people's lifestyle. I just learned that Zec's sister was killed and your daughter was kidnapped."

She shoots that shit straight like she telling me we going to a cookout. My body wants to give out. I stay strong, have'ta act like I knew all this. Can't give her the upper hand. She musta found all this out from Chance. Is he tryna get back at my man? I don't know, they might be beefing you neva know.

"Thanks so much for the info. I knew all that. We was talking about that when you walked up."

"It's one more thing you two probably don't know."

She tells me, I play it off like I knew that too. "I know that as well."

She lets out a load of breath. "Good, that makes me feel better. I know how gangstas work. They hate telling us anything."

"I hear you. On that note, Zec tells me everything. He even told me that you and him used to fuck."

Her eyes get big like she saw a big ass rat.

"That was long ago, girl, nothing there." She tries to immunize it.

"Don't matter. It's what it is, right?" I tell her ass, walking over to him. *She's so fuckin' easy.* I get back to the table.

"What was that about?" He's curious.

"Wouldn't you like to know? Where do you want me to start?" I ask his slow ass.

"Stop playing wit' me. I didn't come all this way for games."

"How about the fact you two fucking."

He's calm as always, and cool. "So what if I hit? That's what all that was she told you? I fucked her? Really, that's what you mad about?"

"I should be, but no I'm mad you didn't tell me our daughter's life is in danger, bitch!"

"Call me a bitch again, hear. I found her. She was in the hospital. I didn't wanna tell you, didn't want you to worry. I know how you get."

"Bet that bitch ass April knows. Your sister, she got killed. Why didn't you tell me, Z. I loved her."

He lowers his head. "I know you did. It's what the fuck it is. Nikki's wit' my Aunt. She's doing her thing wit'a. I took care of the light work. We good."

"Did you find out who was chasing me, trying to take my life?"

"Babe, I have no idea. James got his ears to the ground."

"James, that slime ball nigga. I wouldn't trust his ass as far as I could see'em. My guess is you didn't know he was in on our child getting kidnapped. He works for Andrew."

He sits up. I got his attention now. He glances over at Chance. Chance smiles, giving him a salute.

"James, how she know?"

"The hell if I know. But how would she know any of it, right?" I seal that shit, making sure he takes care of the situation.

"I'ma have'ta go. I love you, D. Take that info back you gave them Boys for real." He kisses me. We say our good-byes. That's the end.

Chapter 27
Zec

I can't believe this shit. My man James, how could he do this shit? That muthafucka, how could he? Not my daughter. I pull up to his shit, turn down my engine, jump out my truck.

Bang. Bang. I bang on his door like the madman I am.

"Yo what up, man? Why you—?"

Cutting his wind short, I jerk his ass up by the collar. I push'em back in his house, kick the door shut with the back of my foot.

"What in the fuck is wrong wit' you, man? How you gon' kidnap my daughter? If I thought it was you behind that shit I would've killed yo ass on the spot when I seen you the other day? Why man, why?" I needed answers. That's why he's still alive.

"Joe, let me explain. It wasn't like that. It was a mistake."

"A mistake? A mistake?! How you make a mistake wit' my daughter then you drugged her, nigga!" I'm getting madder and madder by the second.

"Drugs? Man, I have no idea what you talking about. When I seen they had her I fed her, left to find out how I was gon' get her back to you. I swear. We went to your sister's house to get at Deja, not to get your daughter. It was TD's idea to take her so we could fish out Deja. That was the idea. Then you told me she got popped, I swear."

I let his collar go. "What Chance got to do with this?" I ask.

"Chance, he ain't got shit ta do wit' it as far as I know. This shit is all BMB shit."

I look him over. "Is Chance the head of BMB?"

"Nah, that's Andrew's shit. That's who I work for. I mean, that's who I report to, his weird ass."

"What they doing wit' them kids? Is it a underground sex movement?"

"Hell if I know. I do what they tell me, that's it."

He turns, pulling his shirt up.

"Oh shit," I say out loud, covering my mouth. "What happened to you?"

"This what happens when you make mistakes. They blamed the whole ordeal about your daughter getting saved on me. When they saved your daughter the po-po got the whole mother load. They gave me 100 lashes. That's the highest punishment for the crime."

"James, man, why you stay with them niggaz?" I ask.

A *Classy* THUG

"I been wit'em since 7th grade. They my family. They think I work for you part time. I told him 100 times your just my friend, my boy. I don't know shit you do."

"I believe you, man. What happened wit' Deja? I told y'all to kill'a. I need the insurance money. When my daughter called I panicked. I thought y'all was tryna off her too."

"Man, that nigga Mac fucked up. He hit her car too soon. I told his ass. He didn't listen."

"He did tell me that but he's dead, no need to ask'em. I killed him at my sister's house. I know he was the one that killed her. I could smell his cologne all over her," I tell James.

He looks down at the ground. I put my arms around him.

"C'mon man, we came too far to let this shit get between us."

"Joe, I'm sick of this. I want better. I don't have a wife, children, nothing. I need and want better, man." He looks up at me crying.

"Sit right here, man. It's gon work itself out. Let me make you a drink," I tell his ass.

I walk to the bar, make a sudden about face.

Bloc! One to his left eye. Nigga getting too soft for me. Plus he didn't kill Deja like I ordered his ass. Too many mistakes. 100 lashes, just kill the bitch ass nigga. *He ain't have no purpose in life any ole way,* I tell myself, pouring me a drink, downing it. Then I leave his spot out the back door.

123

Chapter 28
Errica

It's been one month I been out of that joint. I'm happy as hell, living it up. I'm back at the clubs, stripping, doing my thing.

"Lovely?" This girl named Black Beauty calls out.

"Wussup," I answer with a grin running across my pretty face.

"It's a green light asking for you." Green light is a code name for money man.

"I'm on my way," I tell'a. "Where is he?"

"Standing by the bar."

Quickly beating up my face some more, checking my body out in the long length mirror touching up my hair, I exit the dressing room.

Dag on that's Chance standing over in the corner and my money man at the bar. Maybe I can get some money outta both.

I sashay my ass over to Chance first, knowing he got major loot.

"Hey, Chance, where you been? I ain't seen yo ass since that day you picked a sista up."

"Right, right. I been out of town. I told you I be going out of town a lot."

The guy that was waiting on me, my regular, walks over to me.

"Lovely, come over to me when you finish wit' this lame duck."

"Man, you got it. I'on want no problems," Chance feeds back, to my surprise.

My customer puts a crisp Benjamin in my top, then another. He grits on Chance.

Chance smiles, taking a sip from his straw. "That's one of your regulars, huh?" Chance takes notice.

"If you call it that. You have changed. You let him get away with that slick talk."

"Baby girl, I make billions. I don't have time for cat fights. He's a idiot that works for a factory, spending his hard-earned money on pussy. I feel for'em. If I was him I would be upset with life too." He smiles again like shit butter.

Shit like that makes my pussy turn to cream.

"So what brings you by?" I ask, taking the two hundred out my top, stuffing it in my money bag.

"I need your help."

"What you need?"

"I need four unknown bitches. Homeless ones preferred."

"What?"

"Four bitches nobody cares about. Ones that don't have a family."

"Shit, it's a lot of 'em in here."

I call 4 girls over, intro them to Chance. Taking them to the side I tell 'em he wants them for a party, $300 apiece. I lie, don't know why but I did.

Pulling him to the side, I tell 'em what I did. He's ok wit' it.

The girls seem like they down, ask when he want ta do the damn thang. I tell them he's ready to go any time they are. So they go and get ready, preparing. While I'm giving my customer a lap dance, Chance eyeballs me.

Feeling he wants to lace my ears with something, I get up. "I'll be back," I tell my 200-dollar man.

"Hurry back. I'll keep my dick hard," his nasty ass says.

I just look at his horny ass. He watches my butt shake as it bounces moving over to Chance.

"Tell the girls to go outside around back," he tells me.

I relay the intel. They do what's asked.

Going back to Chance feeling like a bell girl, "Ok, Chance, is that it?"

J.J. Jackson

"Yeah, slim. I'ma holla at you tomorrow." He puts a white thick envelope in my top. "Tell 2 short to enjoy you for tonight."

"Chance, you wrong for that," I laugh.

Smiling, putting down his drink, he leaves out the front door.

Making an about face I go to the dressing room, pull the envelope out my top, opening it.

Hot damn! All $100 bills, about 20 of 'em. Damn, whatever he's into wit' them girls I hope he come back and get more.

Chapter 29
Zec

I had to get away from all the mayhem. I take a ride down to the Florida Keys to see Juswa. She said she wanted to go visit her sister to meet her at her home there. I thought it would be a good idea to allow her to meet my daughter. Nikki is a bright girl. We talked about what's been going on the last few days. She said she understood. She says she held her ground even though she was a little scared. I been losing money all around, tending to all this shit. I'm doing something wrong. Don't know what but I gotta get my shit together, regroup, rebuild, do some'em.

"Daddy, it's nice out here. Look at the water." She looks out the window.

"You sho' nuf right about that, baby girl. Nikki, when we get here to my friend's house, don't be talking about mommy, ok."

She looks at me. "Daddy, I'm not five. I know we going to one of your girl's houses. Just like I know Aunt April was your girl. It's sad she's in heaven though."

"You are a big girl. Maybe too big."

Pulling around the corner to Juswa's beach house, I see her fine ass standing on the porch. Honking my horn, she waves us in. I park my truck. Nikki is the first to get out.

"Hi," Nikki walks up to Juswa greeting.

I get our bags out the truck. "You're Nikki, the beautiful one," Juswa tells her.

Nikki smiles. "Why do all daddy's friends say that?"

I could have choked her little ass.

Juswa looks over at me. "Well, Nikki, I'm not your Daddy's friend. I'm his wife to be."

I need a fuckin' drink. I think I made a mistake by bringing her here.

"His wife to be? That sounds crazy. My daddy is already married to my momma."

"Come on, Nikki, let's unpack and get you on the beach with Juswa's God daughter."

"But da—"

I cut her smart ass off. "No but just get in here."

She pouts 'cause I never talked to her like that, but she was blowing up the spot.

Chapter 30

Zec

The next morning the sun shines through the beach house. I enter the room with a serving tray in hand.

"Good morning, sleepy head," I greet Juswa at 10 a.m.

"Good morning," she replies, yawning, stretching, rolling over. "What's this?"

"Some breakfast for the lady of my life. Oh shit, I let the cat out the bag."

"I'm glad you did. I like it." She gives approval.

I set her tray beside her on the bed. "Jus, I want you to know when I'm wit you I feel different. I haven't known you but for a few weeks but it feels like forever, like the shit is right. I really do care for you in my heart. I've been wit' women like my daughter's mother for over 15 years. You're a lot different. I'on know, I said the love of my life. I mean dat shit."

She looks at me wit' them bedroom eyes. "Look over there on my dresser. Bring me that wrapped blue box."

I do what is asked.

"It's for you."

"For me?"

"Yep," she says, looking all serious.

I tear into it.

"A toilet stool?" I question, looking crazed in the face.

She sits up. "Zec, since I met you, you haven't been straight wit' me. I'm very spiritual. I know when people lying, holding back." She shoots it real. I can respect dat.

I get up, taking a seat in the chair next to her bed, feeling like the wind was just knocked out my lungs.

"What you saying, you not feeling dis?" A nigga lost like hell.

"No, not at all. I'm really feeling this. I wanna take it further. I wanna be with you day and night. Hell, I wanna take it all the way but you gotta come clean. Z, who are you? Where you live? Who are the women in your life besides me? When you can tell me that, you can flush all your shit in that toilet. Then we good," she spits.

"What?" Still lost on my end of the spectrum.

"Zec, you have three phones. One blue that never rings; that's probably your women. The white one, that's probably your family line. And the red one, maybe business or Nikki's line. See, I was involved with this guy … he was good to me for six months. Really cared for him. The thing I couldn't take was his lying. I knew it. I allowed it. I said when I leave him, never again. So, Zec—never again. This body, mind, and soul is mines. I love it too much to be played, feel me?"

"Jus, maybe you need to flush some shit too. I see you don't work, but you living in these plush houses. You got them shits all over. Dis like the third one I've been to. Hell—DC, Miami, now the Keys. One mill easy, each." I throw that shit back in her face.

"Say no more. My father is rich. This is his house. He has many more. When you said the name of your real estate company I knew it was real. That's where my father gets his properties."

"I'll take that," I spit. "Who is your father?" I quiz.

"Now you gotta sit back. My father is the head of the A Capon family. I have my mother's last name, Giovanni. He's a good dad, been waiting for me to get married so he can find someone to help wit' the family business. I been scared of the men he sends me 'cause I don't want an Italian macho guy. You have your own. I feel good about you. You not out there like that. Stop looking at me like that. I'm not saying we have to get married. I'm just saying I'm feeling you, I want all cards on the table. You said you wasn't married, your daughter seems to think different though."

I smile. "Jus, I had a girlfriend. She's dead. Nikki's mother, I been wit' since high school. I mess around wit'

strays, not gon lie. Since I been wit' you I been clean, no bitches."

"What is it you do besides real estate?"

"I'm a boss nigga, baby. A street mogul. I don't run the real estate companies. I got a partner, she's like 60 years old but she's good at what she do. We go 60-40. Me 60, her 40."

Putting her pointer finger up, she motions me to come. I slide between her open legs, start kissing her down her neck.

"Daddy?" Nikki says from behind.

"Fuck."

Nikki stays home the next time. My dick was ready for a party.

Chapter 31

Errica

"Coming to the stage is the lovely Black Pearl," the DJ calls through the club.

I make my way to my good client. He be tipping stacks. I can't let them hungry bitches get close to his ass, no way.

"Lovely?" I hear over the loud ass music. I whip my neck around.

"Chance, what his ass want now?" I say in a low voice.

Holding up one finger like I'm excusing myself from church, I signal my client to wait, then I put my hand to my mouth like I'm getting a drink. I make my way to Chance's fine rich ass.

"What up?" I ask, looking over at my client, making sure them thirsty hoes don't hop on'em.

"So we doing it like this?"

"What you talking about?"

"You looking at some off brand while I'm standing in your face?"

"Oh, just securing my property."

He laughs. "Shawdy, you funny as shit."

I turn to him 'cause he's right. I'm being rude. I owe this man my life since it seems he don't want no more of this wet-wet.

"So what brings you in here tonight? You need more girls? What happened to the ones I sent you? I haven't seen them back here?" My nosy ass.

"See, there you go." he says, reaching for his drink. "I need a chick with a baby. Like two babies."

"Chance, what in the fuck you up to these days?" I need to know now.

"What I tell you about getting in my business? I'on be asking you what you be doing wit these broke ass niggaz, do I?"

"Point taken. These dancers named TT and Fuck Me, they got like six kids a piece. TT's kids like 6 months, 1-2-4; and Fuck Me, hers is like 2-6-5-9-10-12."

"Sound like that bitch been fucking for real. They in here tonight?" he asks.

"Yeah."

"See that nigga over there." He points.

"I'on wear glasses, nigga."

He smirks. "Send them to him," he orders, stuffing my top with another envelope. This time a brown one.

"Thanks," I tell his ass, not caring 'cause them bitches wouldn't care about my ass for sho'. "Anything else?"

"Nah, I'll be back tomorrow."

"You know what? You should get wit' Zec. Y'all two together would run the world."

"See, that's yo thinking. The president runs the world. I don't need that headache. Got my own, thanks," he spits, fly like.

"When you gon' come by and give me some of that good ass Back-half-Vietnam dick."

"You got jokes. I gotta head out. Go to your 'client', as you call him." He starts laughing again.

I feel so small—but richer. I go tell my client I gotta go to the restroom. I go in, open the envelope. *OMG!* I count $30,000. *Fuck, I love working wit' his ass!*

Chapter 32

Deja

"Fuck you, bitch. I bet you better not turn that fuckin TV dough."

"What you gon' do if I do? Shit!'

"Turn the bitch and see. I'ma break all yo fuckin fingers. Yo ass won't be sticking them bitches in nobody's pussy tonight, you dike ass bitch."

"I'll show yo ass dike."

As soon as that bitch ran up on the other one, I get ghost. I go to my room, tired of hearing these catty ass bitches box wit' they tongues all day. That fight is over the fuckin TV. I don't get it. A TV we don't even own. That shit is the government's. Who cares? I guess that's how some of 'em do their time. They need to be concentrating on how they gon' get some money when they leave this bitch.

"Excuse me," this girl says, opening my cell door.

"Yes?"

"They calling your name over the speaker. I figured you didn't hear it over all the noise. My name is Pat. They call me Pee."

"Thanks, Pee."

"It's cool. Just didn't want you to miss your visit."

"Oh, you didn't say it was a visit. Thanks."

I get out of bed, hurry to get dressed. This must be Z coming to see my ass. As I get dressed, I think about Pee. She looks just like a stone cold nigga. If I saw her ass on the street I swear I would think she was a nigga.

Rushing over to visit hall, I check in, they give me a light body search. I walk in casting the place.

Saint, what he doing up here? That's right, my cousin told me he was asking about me to send him a visit list. I didn't really think he would fill it out.

I strut my hips over to him.

"Hey, beautiful lady." He stands, wrapping his arms around me.

Now Saint, he is the fuckin man. He's one of them niggaz that lay that game on you so thick you'll kill yourself if you lose'em. Two of his bitches DRA—dead on arrival. He left they asses, they lost they muthafuckin mind. I thanked God I never messed wit' his ass. They say his dick so damn good, eight inches of pure pleasure. His tongue game is not to be fucked wit'. He takes the F outta the word fine. Just looking at his ass making my pussy cat willow.

A *Classy* THUG

"Saint, I didn't think you would really come."

"Baby girl, you know my word Fendi when I say I'ma do. I do, you heard."

"Where you been?" I ask.

"I been working hard. Working for UPS now, loading shit, feel me?"

"I bet you are." I smirk.

"You know I am. When you rising up outta this peace, young?"

"Man, I got a little time ta go. I'm hoping next year."

"Join some classes, work out, get a job, read, make time go fast. Stick to your own. Stay out of drama, do what them folks tell you ta do. Wit' dat dumb shit said, how's the flip side of you holding?" he asks.

Whoo I just love his ass. Am I dreaming? Is his ass sitting here smiling, showing them golds for real?

"What flip side? Who you talking 'bout?" I know but I want to make sure.

"C'mon, shawdy—you, Zec. Y'all come too far, you heard."

"Saint, that mutha ain't shit. I'm in here, he ain't brought my daughter to see me—"

"Word?"

"Let me finish. He ain't doing shit. His hoe died. He used to send her up to see me." He jerks his neck back, balling up his top lip. "Yeah, his other hoe ... he had her taking care of our daughter—"

141

He cuts me off, laughing.

"What's so funny?"

"You, shawdy."

"What?"

"You still claiming Z is the father. You know he ain't the daddy." He laughs.

"Saint, you play too much."

"No that's you, baby girl. Chance that girl father all day long. She even got them Vietnamese eyes like'em. I remember the day y'all got down in Suitland's bathroom. That bell rung, y'all crazy niggas had me as the lookout."

I laugh. "How you remember that?"

"I'on know. I guess in some type of way I wished it was me."

I blush like he kissed my cheek.

"You right, dough. I always thought she was Chance's. I was too scared to tell him. Didn't want him to think I was trying to trap'em. So many girls was after him. After that one time it was a wrap."

"Life fucked up sometimes. Now I know why Zec gettin' you dough."

"Why, Saint? Why would Z do some shit like that to me? The mother of his child?"

"Five mill on your head, ma."

"'Cause I ratted the supplier out?"

"Exactly."

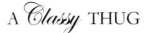
I turn my head, tears flowing fast. I tried to stop'em, they just came.

"Don't cry, ma. Don't let these crackas see you cry. Get your life together, make it up outta here."

He wipes my tears with napkins 'cause they just wouldn't stop. *I have to get out of here and I know how,* I'm thinking.

"Baby girl, I don't think you have to worry 'bout him, dough. I hear that nigga in love wit' another chick."

Those words leap from his mouth like he sent crabs in my belly. Getting up, I run to the restroom, throw up what I didn't eat. Officer Thompson comes in the bathroom checking on me. I told her I was ok, just not feeling too well, heard some fucked up news. She left me to mourn. Cleaning my face, I walk back to Saint.

"You gon be a'ight, ma?"

"Yeah Saint, thanks."

"No thanks. I had to let you know. You Ronda's cousin and an old friend. I lace some honey on your books. Shit should last for like two months. I told Ronda to shoot you my 10. If you need anything, call. I'ma hit you back tomorrow dough, doing some work this way. I'ma stand by you, ma. I got yo back for real dough."

I reach over, touching his arm.

"Thanks, Saint, thanks. Tell me something dough. How you find all this out?"

"I used to holla at the chick he jive blowing wit'. We still talk somewhat. She was whistling his name in my ear. She told me her peeps told her dat shit. She don't know I know you dough.

"Why y'all fall out, you and the girl he seeing?"

"She was on some ole gotta know er' thing. She pretty but not that pretty, feel me?"

"Thanks again," I tell'em.

"For the record, that shit he pulling is dirty shady dough. But you not no better, feel me? Erase dat snitching shit, ma. That shit ain't gon' fly. Do shit on the up and up. Always know the man behind the gun ain't always the one pulling the trigga. Watch yo'self, feel me?"

I nod my head. He lifts up, hugs me.

"I got you this trip ma, for sho."

For some reason I didn't wanna let his ass go. I always liked him. But scared he was gon' rip my heart out like he just did.

Life ain't easy.

Chapter 33

Zec

Two weeks pass, I'm still down here wit' Juswa. I gotta pull myself together, get back on my square. I gotta go, me and Nikki. I know she wanna see her mother. She's been talking about her. I owe her mother that much since she pulled her testimony back. I wanna take shorty Juswa to DC wit' me.

I skip steps, pulling up on Juswa.

"Baby, what you doing in here?"

"Cooking. What it look like, boy?" she smiles.

"Baby, I gotta get Nikki back. I gotta take her ta see her mother. You know how that shit go."

A frown grows on her face.

"What's wrong?" I coo.

"I just don't want you to go. I'ma miss you so much. I love you, baby."

"Come correct. Don't be jelly. It's you I want, not her. She got years. She's my daughter, feel me?" Pressing my forehead to hers. "You know what they say—the closest get the mostess."

"They do, huh? I know. Poppy wants to see you. He's coming to DC next week so you two can make arrangements to meet up."

"Whatever you say." *Boy can I wait,* I think.

"You and Nikki come eat before you hit the road."

"Nikki?" I call out.

"Right here daddy, dang," her smart ass says.

"Sit down. Eat."

She sits.

"Mrs. Giovanni you can cook."

"Call her that one mo again, hear." I flash her bad ass a mug shot.

She rolls her eyes. I swear this girl needs some get right but I'm a man, can't put my hands on'a.

After we eat I say my goodbyes. Me and Nikki hit the road. All she talks about is getting back to her mother. I'm thinking why did I put a contract out on her head? She been there for me. But I owe it to the man that's been feeding me, the man that let me in on the dope game. Why couldn't she keep her mouth shut, why?

A few hours later we make it to DC. My guts start bubbling. It feels like stuff ain't right. I drop her off at my aunt's joint then dip over to my joint. I go in, take a shower, dress in my street gear, put in a few calls, then my last call is to lil man.

"What's cooking dough?" he answers.

"Nutten, what up wit'cha," I flow.

"Shit man, dat nigga Andrew out here getting all the paper. He be rolling. Nigga riding out in a Rolls they ain't even come out wit' yet. I seen that shit in the magazine labeled 2018. Fuck, a year away. I saw his ass when I was in Cali. He'on bang that shit out here. He be on them Honda's like his ass broke when his ass in town," he say, riding his nuts like he his best cheer leader.

"He doing it the right way dough. Everybody gotta get theirs they own way. Ain't they pushing underground pussy? That shit always sell, and it neva goes on sale," I base back to'em.

"I couldn't tell you. My pussy is this dope, you feel?"

"I feel you man, I do. But if that shit sells like dat, I need ta change my profession. What you think?" I remark.

We laugh.

"Where you been anyway?" he utters.

"You ain't been answering your phone and shit. You hitched or some'em? Yeah, so you and ole girl finally—"

I interject. "Me and another girl, not Deja."

"Man you lost me. What in the entire fuck is going on?"

"I'll explain that shit to you when I see you."

"So what you doing wit' Chance? We still at war?" my man asks.

"Nah, man. He gave me some good info so he gets to live a little longer."

"I feel you on that."

"You handling business," I note.

"We taking some losses since you know they shut 3 of our blocks down, but all in all we hanging."

"How much a week now?"

"100,000."

"Fuck, we way down. I gotta get us back up. No worries. We gon' be back on top soon," I assure him.

"We know you got us. You always come through."

"For sho'. We gon' make it, believe dat. On er' thing I love," I assure.

"I know, man. Look, I'ma holla at you on the South side. I got some shit I gotta do," he shoots.

"Ok man, holla later," he says.

"$100,000 a week? What the fuck we gon' do with that?" I say out loud driving mad as fuck.

Chapter 34

Zec

"Shit really gettin outta hand, man."

"What you mean? What's wrong now?" my brother from another motha asks.

"Man, shit wasn't supposed ta go down like it is, that's all."

"You sound stressed. Won't you come through?" Sam, my father's son by another woman, states.

"Thanks. I think I'll take you up on it. I'ma have'ta hit you up lata dough," I breathe in the phone.

"Bet, nigga. Get some rest, dough. You sound like you need it," he counsels. He's a square dude.

"I'ma do that as soon as I hit yo joint."

"Like I said, anytime man. Until you come through."

"Until then. One," I feed back, ending the call.

Walking up to James's mother's door sticking my cell phone in my pocket, I ring the doorbell.

"Coming!" I hear her yellin'. Opening the door: "Oh it's you. Hi, Z. Come in."

"I don't need ta come in. I'm just here to pick up some'em that's in your backyard, that's all." I minimize the shit.

"Oh … ok. By all means take your time back there. James not here. I haven't heard from that boy in a minute now. You know how you boys do."

"Oh if I see him I'll tell'em to slide through. But he knows I was coming by today," I lie.

"No problem. I know how you two are."

"I'll come back when I'm done," I inform.

"I'll be in the kitchen cooking."

"Got you."

I hop the fence, move the play house. *Man, this is why you never tell your right hand what your left doin'.* Just what I came for, money wrapped in plastic. I go pull my truck up. I start loading the treasure.

Damn, dis nigga been rippin' my ass off fo' real or doing shit on the side, one, I think to myself while putting the money in my truck. When I'm done I knock back on the front door. She opens it.

"Did you get what you came for?" she questions like she wasn't watchin'.

"Yes, ma'am. I did this for you."

She looks at the bundle of money wrapped in plastic. "That's ok. I don't want no blood money."

"Mrs. Harris, dis money don't know where it came from."

"No it don't, son. But I do."

"Suit yourself. Good seeing you." I give her a hug, drop the money in the mail box that hangs by her front door. "Mrs. Harris, it's right there if you need it."

Her lips part into a happy face. "I love you, Zecman." Closing her door.

Only if she knew she's gon' need it, unless she has death insurance on her one and only son.

I get in my truck, head to April's mom's, who's in pain right about now 'bout her daughter's demise. Her death was on the news, her face blown off. The only reason she was identified is because of her ID in her purse. I pull up to her house. *Damn it's more cars out here then at the clubs on a Friday night.*

I park my truck, walk in. *Damn it's a lot of people in dis bitch.* I hunt for her mother, unidentified pussy everywhere, their eyes all over me too. *Not interested.* There she go. I spot her ass sitting on the sofa in her living room. Money hungry bitch. I can't stand'a, but she is April's mom, plus I owe April dis much. She locks eyes wit' mines.

"Hi, Zecman," she greets wit' a smiley face that says *give me some dead presidents.*

"Hey, Mrs. Oman, sorry about April."

"No, son, I'm sorry for you. I know how much you loved her."

"That I did. I loved her ta death," I tell her as we embrace.

"Have a seat," she demands.

"Nah, I got a lot ta do," I explain, short sightin' the 20 people checking my mouth for cavities. "You need anything?" I put out there.

"No … well, maybe you know her burial cost a lot of pocket money. Were you there? I don't remember you being there that day."

Like a square, I tell'a, "I was out of town, sorry. I couldn't take it. You know how that goes, right? Is it somewhere we can cap some privacy?"

Getting the hint she quickly slips her small hand in mines. "Excuse me y'all, I'll be right back."

Her eyes are red; I gather from crying. She leads me to her room. I stand in front her, pulling out 10 bands. I hand them to'a.

"Oh this is too much, Zecman."

"Take it. I owe her that much. It's the least I can—"

"Grandma."

I look over her shoulders as this boy calls her, cutting me off and taking me by surprise.

"I thought we was alone," I spit.

"No worries. He's April's son."

My heart beats through my fuckin shirt. My eyes start blinking, my head takes flight. Keeping shit on the up and up, "That youngsta looks just like my ass. How old is he?" I manage to let out.

"13."

I look at her mother, then at him.

"I know, right. He's the spitting image of you. She didn't want to tell you. She said you didn't want any children so she kept him here with me."

I don't have words. I mean I just killed my son's mother. I take a seat.

"Are you ok, Zecman?"

"Give me a sec."

He looks over at me. "Are you my dad?"

"Yes he is, son," Mrs. Oman lets out.

The youngen walks up to me.

"Are you ok?" he asks.

"I'm good," I say, thinking, *I got a boy—a boy no one told my ass about. How do you hide a whole child?*

Getting a grip on myself, I man the fuck up. "Mrs. Oman?"

"I'm right here."

"If he needs anything you call me. Anything," I spit with cold eyes, pissed as a mug. Giving him full attention, "Son, what's your name?"

153

"Zecman Jr."

I smile. "That you are."

His eye light up.

"Can I come get him from time ta time." Getting permission from his grandmother.

"Of course you can." She's thinking about how much money she gon' get.

"Tomorrow 10 a.m. Have him ready."

"Yay!" he says, hugging me around the waist like he's been waiting for this all his life.

I hug him back, thinking, *A fuckin son … Damn, April, why didn't you say some'em? Deja was right—April was one sneaky bitch.*

Chapter 35

Zec

"Tiny, man, can you believe dis shit? April had my seed, man. She had a boy. He's a Jr. How she hold some shit back like that from a nigga?" I grieve to my man.

"I can't tell you that. The most important thing is that you keep your head up, keep up with reality," he says as we chop things up in my game room.

"You gon' meet lil man tomorrow. I'ma go pick'em up. Ma dukes say he jive smart. That's a good thing 'cause his mother had rocks for brains. Who holds back a whole child? Man, where they do that shit at?"

"Women. They think different than us. See, we wanna conquer pussy. When they get hit, they think up the road like marriage. Speaking of marriage, where you and ole girl having the wedding?" He's got jokes.

"Who said anything about marriage?" I feed back.

"Y'all all in love, right? You be spending hella time with the lady."

"Now you really being funny. That's why I'm killing yo ass in this game. Take that, nigga," I tell him, blasting his man away.

"All I'm saying is at some point in your life you gotta slow it down, that's all," he articulates.

"You right. And at some point you gotta speed up and find you some stay-at-home pussy," I speak out loud and clear.

"I set myself up for that. How your business going? You ain't really been acting yourself, it seems."

"You ain't never lied. Shit been going duck since my man Kurt died. We used to get that money. When I find out who killed him, it's over for they ass for sho. All the po-po want is a fuckin pay off. Them niggaz ain't got time for real police work. In this case I'ma be the police," I assure this while I kill his ass on this Grand Theft Auto shit. "Boom! Nigga you dead!" I yell, standing up walking to my stash. I grab a handful of ganja. "You want some?" I ask before rolling.

"Hell yeah, bring that shit man," he say wit' a cheesy.

"My man." I roll, we puff pass.

"You think it's too soon for me to be getting down wit' Jus?" I say, coughing and shit.

"Nigga, it's yo life. You gotta live that shit the way you see fit."

"Thanks, man. That's all I needed to hear." My cell buzzes. "Hello?"

"Hello, Mr. Washington, this Juswa's father."

I sit straight up. "How you doing, Sir." I show respect.

"I'm doing well. May I ask you to come to your front door?"

"My front door?"

"Yes, son, the door of your home."

I look at Tiny, who's looking at me like *what's going on*. I put two fingers to my eyes, letting him know to look out. He grips my Glock, walks with me to the front door. I open it.

"You want me to come to your limo, or you coming in?"

"Come to my limo. I assure you nothing is going to happen to you or your friend."

I walk to his limo. His driver opens the door to let me in.

Taking a seat by him, he speaks, "Son, I know this visit is a surprise to you. I also know you and my only daughter are planning a wedding. I don't care who she marries. It's her life, her right. I do have a problem with your child's mother, Deja. She's bringing on troubles for the families. Being a man of businesses, you know we can't afford trouble."

"What's she doing now?" I respond.

"She's due to testify on one Geo Gotti. This we can't allow. Both families work together, if you follow what I'm saying."

"How do she know anything about that family?"

"Your supplier, he's an accession of ours. She's turning on him. This poses a problem for us. Mr. Antoine is a courier for the Gotti family. We are the suppliers for them. Do you see how this will become a domino effect?"

"I see. She told me she was backing off dough."

"As of 2 a.m. this morning she gave her statement to one Detective Hurries."

"What?!" I'm lost, pissed, fucked up.

"Ok, Sir. I'll go see her in the morning."

"Thanks, and welcome to the family," he tells me. "Tell her we will get her out, to hold tight if she drops this. Son, I know you will be a great leader in our family as well. You used to work so hard for me. Juswa spoke of you when she was a child and now you two are dating. That is something, isn't it?"

When she was a child? The little girl that was always looking over the rails when I came to the house? Jessie. Lil Jessie. She grew up. She don't look the same and she's older than me, I think to myself.

"I guess one day you will be back with me. This time you will be working with me. You and my daughter, she is fond of you. She speaks highly of you. I know your loyalty. I would just have to get to others to learn who you are."

A *Classy* THUG

My ass is smiling on the inside. If I can get with them, money boy money no worries my black ass will be set, my kids. Fuck Deja. I gotta look out for me. My mind is flowing right now.

"Thanks, Sir. Know I will take care of Juswa to the end of my breathing days."

"I'm sure, son. My driver has something for you when you exit the car. Thanks again." He nods to his hangmen who gives one knock for the driver to let me out. I get out, he hands me a package. I stand watching the car as it pulls off.

"What was that about?" Tiny asks, standing in my doorway.

"My heart is in my shoes." When I get in the house, I open the package. "What the fuck? A gun, money, lots of money wrapped up." I tell Tina what he said. He steps back, giving me the strong eye.

"Man, he want you to knock Deja off when she get out. He paying you to take care of your child's mother. What you gon' do?"

I stand glaring at Tiny, then all the money.

What do I do? I think to myself. *I'll talk to her. She's gotta make this right. When I get her out she can move to another country with Nikki. Yeah, that's it.*

Chapter 36

Errica

"Hey you, I can't believe you wanted to meet me here and not in the club."

"Why would you say that?" Chance says, taking a seat at the restaurant table across from me.

"You always be coming to the Penthouse, so I was like I guess you don't trust me enough to see me outside of the joint."

"You hungry?" he asks.

"Not really. Just ate. I gotta go to work in 3 hours. Don't like to eat before going to work. You know, don't wanna be farting on niggaz."

He laughs, showing them deep dimples wit' them pretty teeth.

"So what you bring me here for?" I'm curious.

"Why it had to be a reason?"

J.J. Jackson

He thinks I'm dumb for real, so I spell it out for'em. "Chance, you got me out only to make me your slave bitch. It's cool though. You have me picking out these bitches for God knows what. Hell, TT mom called the club looking for her daughter. She said the kids and TT been missing. She said it's not like TT not to call her. So whatever you convincing these hoes to do after I send them to you, they not coming back. It's like you sending them to the point of no return, 'cause the 1st set of ladies I sent to you ... Them bitches, neva seen'em again. I know I'm here so I must be doing something right."

He leans back in his seat, observing my face. "You on the right track. I know I can trust you 'cause when I come in the club I'm not being greeted by the police. I been checking your moves, making sure you not tryna blow the spot up. E, I'm real. I don't take chances. When I roll the dice it's a hit every time. I know you used to fuck with my boy Andrew. I brought your name up to him, told him I wanted to make a move wit' you business-wise. He vouched for you for real. He laid low while you did the 4 years test. I know you asking why. When you was working for him you was working for me. Drew don't even know what goes on behind the scenes. He can only speculate. Let me put it to you like this: What I'm running is a multi-billion dollar business, nonstop money. Am I the head? Yes. I deal with all kinds of people from all over the world. That's how I made the move to get

162

you out so fast. I didn't put my name on no visit list. I pulled strings to get in to see you. That's how my life rolls. You wit' me?"

Damn, he spit that shit out so smooth without breathing.

"Keep going," I tell his ass, wondering now what I'm into.

"I need your work. E, I know you'll be a great accent to the team." He stares at me.

"Chance, what am I getting into?"

"Smart girl. I need you to get me product—men, women, children. You walk the track, play the clubs all over where I tell you. You send them to the mouthpiece that I supply for you. That's all you, just point'em out and we do the rest. The tricks—you put drugs in their drinks; we take over from there. "

"Chance, what you into? You can tell me, you know you can."

"I thought you'd never ask. Come with me."

I jump in the truck wit' his fine ass.

163

Chapter 37
Zec

I race my ass to the prison, flooring it. *This girl, she gon' fuck er'thing up for my future.* I sign in, go to a table, wait. Thirty minutes later her fine ass comes through the door.

"Hey you." She's smiling.

"Fuck dat 'hey you' shit. What the fuck I tell you, D, what?" I fire on her ass.

"Back the fuck up, nigga. What you talkin 'bout?"

"Didn't I tell yo ass ta stand the fuck down on that rat shit? Now the mob tryna gangsta yo ass. I told ya dumb ass."

"First of all I don't give a fuck about you, the mob, who eva. I gotta do what's right for me and my child. You and them what eva you call'em can go to hell. My daughter is first, do you hear that?!"

Her ass so stupid. What I see in her ass?

"D, what you tryna do? Huh? You tryna get Nikki killed? Huh, what?" I throw my hands in the air, giving it to her straight.

"Z, let me tell you this. Listen really good. If anybody touch a hair on my baby's head, I'll personally kill they asses. Know this."

My eyes circle her face. It's something different about'a. What, I can't put my finger on it dough. She looks relaxed, happy. Something's not right.

"D, who you seeing?"

"Nigga, don't worry about what I'm doing. You just relay my messages. Oh and that bounty you got on my head—bitch, they betta come correct."

"D, I'on have no bounty on your head. Who told you that faulty shit?"

"Zec, kiss my ass."

I push up out the chair. "It's your life. I warned your stupid ass."

Rising up slowly like some Queen, "No, you the stupid one. I'm the one that's gon' show you just how stupid you are."

I look back. "So what you sayin'? You gon rat me out too?"

Seductively she smiles then gives my ass a wink. "See you on the flip side, nucca." She disappears behind the door.

What in the fuck got in her? When is she getting out? Is she really ratting them niggaz out? *Fuck'a*, are my words, walking out the double glass doors to my ride.

Chapter 38
Zec

Driving down the highway I eye this envelope Jus put on my passenger seat the other day. Opening it:

My love I wrote this for you ...

I have been told that ... I am not supposed to want you. I'm not supposed to care for you yet I spend all my time dreaming of all that we could share,

I'm not supposed to think of you or wonder where you've been but no matter how hard I fight, the thoughts of you always sneak in without me knowing, I'm not supposed to yearn so always wishing you were here but hunger for your voice I long to draw you near. I'm not supposed to need you. I know these things, I do, I want to fulfill my parents' wishes and yet I can't help myself because I'm falling in love with you.

Damn, I Love her so much. My heart drains for her. Setting the poem down, I park, get out, walk up to Mrs. Colman's front door. With my heart weighing heavy, I ring the doorbell.

"Coming," her voice rings through the door.

She opens the door, lets me in.

"Hi mom, what you up to?"

"Oh nothing. Come in Zecman."

I walk in and shut the door behind me.

"I miss Deja," she says. "I so wish she was here right now."

"I know. You'll see her soon. I put dat on er thing I own."

"I know. I love both of you," she tells me as she drains her soup that's in her pot on her stove.

I stop talking, she turns around.

"Oh no Zecman!" she yells. "Wait, why?!" she adds with fear running across her face.

"I gotta do this."

"Why? I've known you for so long!"

"That's why it's so hard," I tell'a, pointing my .44 towards her face. My focus become blurry, my eyes start blinking. *I gotta do it*, I tell myself.

She closes her eyes in prayer.

Bloc! One to her brain.

A *Classy* THUG

"Damn, Deja, why you have'ta go and be a rat!" I say out loud, leaning in making sure my work is sealed.

I leave her house, hop back in my truck.

See, when I left D today I went past my girl Juswa's joint, trying to get shit off my mind. We was kicking it, having fun, when her father appeared at her front door unannounced. He was happy to see me dough. Coming in, pulling me to one of the many rooms he enlightens me on Deja's little scam. He also told me it's costing him lots of dead heads, lawyers cover up, etc. They are also tryna say he may be the person that murdered Kurt's wife; it's out of my hands. I had to send Deja a message. If she was out here I would've killed her too. I hate rats—and ta think my daughter's mother, my ride or die, is one of 'em. *You do the fuckin crime, you do the fuckin time,* are my thoughts no madda how it hurts. Maybe it was part my fault. *I should've been there for'a more but it was her fuck up, not mines,* I tell myself, driving down Suitland Parkway. I can't seem to get Deja's mom's scared face out my mind.

Chapter 39
Errica

"I don't know why you making me wear this mask over my eyes. If you trust me to go where eva it is you taking me, what's the difference?" I ask Chance as we ride along.

"This way if you wanna pull out you won't know where I took you. We here now so you can take your mask off."

I take off the mask. "Can I have my watch back now?" I ask him. He took that too so I wouldn't know how long it took us to get here, but I remembered I left the restaurant at 6 p.m. It's dark as hell. I know we been driving for like 5 hours or more. I gotta drain my main vein at that.

"What is this big ass building out here in East fuck?" I petition.

"This where it all happens."

We get out, he presses a code into a number pad that's mounted on the side of the door building. The door slides open.

J.J. Jackson

"After you," he tells me.

I walk in. A lady is coming towards us in an all blue jumper.

"Hello, Mr. Tate," she says.

Chance nods his head towards her.

We go on the elevator. He presses 15. I guess that's the 15th floor. From the outside it looks like it's like 20 floors or more.

"After you." He's such a man.

"We walk down this long ass hall full of what looks like offices, but I can't see in. We stop in front these double doors.

"Are you sure you want to ride wit' me, be my right hand go getta? Speak now. It's not too late to turn back."

"Chance, stop playing with me. You act like you got some top spy shit going on. Like I gotta leave home for life."

"Nah, ain't like dat. But are you in or not?"

I look him dead in his fine ass face. "I said I would do what you need me to do. But how much is the pay?" I quiz. All the rest is gravy. The money is what makes the sense to me.

"Dat depends on how much product you bring me. I'll pay you by the month. $200G's."

Automatically my pussy gets wet. "Chance, no matter what's behind that door I'm in."

"Ok."

172

A *Classy* THUG

He puts some codes in, presses his thumb against the panel. The door pops open.

Taking two white coats off a hanging rack, "Here put this on."

I do what is asked. "This not gon' work. You gotta get me a sexy coat. This shit too big."

He laughs.

Turning the knob to the inner door, a brisk of cold air hits my ass. Now I know why I had to put the coat on. It feels like I just walked into a freezer.

We walk over to a glass window. He presses a red button. The blue glass window turns clear. I look in. I lose my breath. Nothing he could've said could have prepared my ass for this.

"My God Chance what the fuck!" I bend over, throw up on the floor, coughing. I feel like I'ma faint. I need to get out. I look up at Chance who's standing looking at me with cold eyes. I think, *Who in the hell is this man, this fine ass boyish looking man?* He's mad. Then $200G's enter my dome.

I straighten my shit up, stand tall. He hands me a napkin to wipe my mouth.

"Don't get close though. I know your breath stink. Don't worry about the mess I'll get someone to clean it up."

I look in one more time. I see TT's face. She has tubes running into her body while this man dressed in all blue takes her organs out!

I helped her die, but I want to know more so I ask, "Where are her children?"

He takes me to another section. I look through the window; it's 6 babies being operated on. Looks like they're being saved. Doctors putting body parts in them, table after table.

"So this is the billion dollar business you was talking about? This is why you're in and out of the country?" I ask.

"Yep. Do you still want in?" he asks.

"Hell yeah. I wanna do whatever it takes to get on your level." All I see is the money. Green drives me, not niggaz no more.

He takes me to the back side of the building. We stand on a catwalk overlooking a lobby where men and women wait to see if their loved ones' organs accept the new organs from the donors. It's sad—all the way around these people pay for a black market organ, knowing people are being killed to save the ones they love.

"Chance, how much do these people pay?"

"Most of them are in the club. They pay by the year. Three mill—that covers their whole family. So if your father gets lung cancer or something like that, they can come here; we'll give them a new lung. They live longer," he explains.

"Who thought of this shit?" I ask.

"Me. When I went to see my father a few years ago in Vietnam, they do it there on a small scale so I started doing it overseas. It worked. I brought it here. That was all she wrote. Now I do it all over the world."

"Now that's what I call hustling," I tell him, thinking this some really high tech shit.

Chapter 40
Deja
The Next Day

"Mrs. Colman, you have a visit," the C.O. calls over the inter-com. After hearing all that bad news, I kinda got in a slump, but all in all it's not that bad like I thought it would be. It beats being in county jail. I got a big ass corner bedroom. I buy all the food I want from the kitchen Contraband of course. The officers are laid back. I get to see a fight between lovers every week, it seems. I learn how to knit; that's some-thing I didn't know how to do. I've been knitting Nikki stuff, sending it to her. I mean I been on my grind as well, tryna get the hell up outta here 'cause it ain't nutten like home.

Ok I'm ready. Nikki's aunt didn't tell me she was bring-ing her this weekend. "Ole well, I'm happy she did," I say to me, walking to the visit hall.

I get there. The C.O. writes down everything I have on. She runs her hands over my entire body. I feel invaded every time. This part I hate about visit. But it's worth it when it comes to my baby girl.

I flash her a smile when she's done. She opens the door to the visit hall. I look around. "Wow!" I say out loud.

It's not Nikki, not that fucked up ass Zec, but it's Chance looking fine as always in his crisp white Tee, crisp blue jeans, butter Tims gold chain, his face trimmed just right and that pinky ring, you know it seals the deal my pussy remembers.

I walk over to him, taking a seat.

"You wasn't expecting me, I know."

"No, I thought it was my child."

"Saint told me you need some help getting the hell outta this camp."

"He did?" I throw out there.

"I'm here, ain't I?"

"You sound bitter about something."

"Why you ain't tell me?"

I look him over. "Tell you what?"

"Now you gon' play dumb."

"What?" I really don't know what he's talking about.

"Nikki, your child. Who's the father?"

I pause. I don't know what to do so I keep shit real.

"She looks like you. I think she's yours, but I was with Zec, you was with Roseland," I remind his ass.

He smiles. "You funny. So when you gon' tell that nigga?"

"As soon as I get out. It's so much going on right now. I can't tell him just yet. I fear for my daughter—"

He breaks in. "I know everything that's been going on. I sent Errica over to tell you that stuff that day. I was here visiting her, remember."

I give the puppy eyes. I hold my head down in shame.

"Look at me," he demands.

I lift my head.

"I got you. Saint told me er thing. I got you."

"What will I be selling my soul for?" I ask 'cause you gets nothing for free.

"For nothing. Shawdy, I been loving you since that day. You broke my heart, you did. Today I can sit here and say this mushy stuff. I want you. I understand if the feeling ain't the same."

"Can we work on getting me out of here first, to Nikki?" I say, still looking like a wet dog.

"We can. That I can do."

"Thanks," I tell him.

We talk about some serious shit. Then it's time for him to go.

"You should be hearing from my lawyer soon," he says.

"Chance, thanks for not being mad. Thanks for believing in me."

"No doubt, Ma. Hold that pretty head up," he says, giving me a hug. It feels so good to feel loved again.

Chapter 41
Deja

"Mrs. Colman? The chaplain wants you to come to her office," Officer Thompson comes to my room announcing. I just got back off my visit with Chance, tired as a mug.

I wonder what she could want with me. I don't even know her, my mind continues to wonder, moving through the compound to her office.

I stand outside her door.

"Mrs. Colman, come in," she utters.

I sit in front of her desk. "State your Reg number for me please."

"51198-007," I call out.

"That's it. Mrs. Colman I'm sorry to tell you, your mother was murdered two days ago."

"My mother? Not my mother, you have the wrong person," I tell her, knowing she can't be right.

"Yes, your mother. Your brother, Eric Colman, called today."

"*OOOOOOOOh nooo!*" I scream, falling to my knees. My whole body feels like it's about to pop. She holds me in her arms, rocking me back and forth until I calm down some.

"Are you ok now?"

I nod yes.

"Let me walk you to your unit where you can get some rest." That she does.

Everyone is looking at me. I feel like I'm in the Twilight Zone.

"Deja, you ok? You alright?" some ask. "What happened to you?" some of the nobodies ask. Then somebody takes me by my arm.

"I got'a chaplain."

"Ok, call me if you need me."

"Yes, ma'am," the person says.

When I get to my room I throw up in the commode over and over.

"I'm sorry," Deja Pee says, who's been down for 35 years for trafficking dope and 5 bodies. We became kinda close. She's so smart and funny. She don't take to too many people but she took to me as soon as she saw me.

People are gathered around the door, acting like they care for real. They just being nosy as fuck.

"All y'all excuse us," Pee lets out.

"Deja, you want me to stay?" someone asks.

"No, Pee here, thanks." I keep shit real even though my head is fucked up right now.

Closing my door, Pee sits me on my bunk. "What happened?" she asks.

"They killed my mother."

"They? Baby, who is they?" she asks.

"The mob."

"The mob?" she retorts. "Why?"

"I don't know but hey killed her." I burst out crying again.

"You got to calm yourself down before you get sick." She takes me in her arms after I'm calm again.

"Now why would they have a reason to kill your mother?" She gets back to the 21 questions.

"I did a rule 501k," I tell her, wiping my eyes with tissue.

"Oh shit, you ratted them out?"

"No, my husband right hand used to sell dope. He got killed, so to lessen my time I ratted him out."

"Oh shit, it probably trickled back to his supplier," she gives wisdom.

"I know it did. I told them about the supplier too."

"Why would you do that? You put the gun to your head and anybody in your family."

183

"I thought I would be ok in here. My daughter, she's got her father but his fucking ass ain't shit either."

"Do her father know all this?" she puts out there.

"Yeah, he came trying to get me to take it all back. He told me the mob was being looked at because of what I said to the FEDs."

"Let me ask you this: Do the man that's dead and your man have the same supplier?"

"No. At least I don't think so." I hunch my shoulders, looking at her blowing my nose.

"Deja?"

"Yeah?"

"Baby girl, I hate to tell you this but your baby father killed your mother."

"No, he wouldn't do that," I tell her, assured.

"Baby, don't be fooled. If his right hand man's supplier knows it was you, then they done talked to yo baby daddy. Girl, he gone do what he gotta do to silence you."

"But it's too late. I got my sentence reduced."

"You can tell'em you made it all up, or it's gon' be more bodies. Don't I know."

"Pee, he would never kill his child. You think he would kill my child?"

"Deja, don't be fooled. He will kill his own mother for the game, depending on how deep in he is. From the sound of it he's in deep. Believe me, I've ate, breathed, and shit the game."

"You know him, Pee?"

"Girl, don't know'em, don't wanna." She holds me tight in her arms as I continue to use her shoulder to cry on.

Chapter 42
Deja
2 weeks later

"How is my girl doing? Y'all ain't been up here in like for-ever," I sing, taking a seat at the round white table in visit hall.

"I know ma. I been so busy. Me and daddy been going everywhere," Nikki giggles.

"Everywhere, huh?"

"Yeah we went to Walt Disney World for the 10th time," she informs me, rolling her eyes towards the back of her head while playing with my ID tag that hangs from my neck at all times.

"But did you have fun?" I ask.

"Yep, it was me, Unc Cee and Jr."

"Who is Jr?" I look over at Z's aunt who's playin' like she don't hear shit, hiding her face behind a fuckin *People* magazine knowing good and well she'on read shit.

"Jr. You know mamma, Daddy's son."

The bottom of my feet automatically turn hot. My head throbs for real. I know my child didn't say daddy's son. I play it off like all other times I had to.

"Oh, Jr," I say, darting my eyes from Nikki to her Aunt. "Nikki?"

"Ye ... ssss?" she answers, holding her head sideways,

"How old is Jr. now?"

"13, I think."

That's close with Nikki's age. That hoe ass bitch, are my thoughts.

"Mom, him and daddy look just alike. But he's kinda slow though."

"Slow?" I repeat.

"He don't know nutten about the game. Daddy have to tell him everything. People gon' get over on him really fast. He don't even know what bands mean."

I laugh. My child so street smart. I'on like it but Zec said he'on won't no grimy ass nigga playin'a, so it is what it is.

"Nikki, go get me some Starburst."

"Got you." I give her money, she runs off.

"Marsha, so you know about all this?"

Closing the magazine, "I'on get into you and my nephew business. I got my own man problems. I bring Nikki up here, do what I can for her. As far as you and Zec, that's

y'all shit, not mines. So don't put out the fish line 'cause I'm not gon' bite."

"I never liked you," I tell'a, thinking out loud.

"The feelings are mutual," she says, picking her magazine back up.

Here comes my little baby girl looking like her father too.

Chapter 43

Listening to my message from Midget say he seen Deja brother sporting a 2018 Benz Coupe, now I know dis nigga owes me so I put in a call to'em.

"Hello?"

"Yo Eric, where my money nigga?"

"Who dis?"

Now dis nigga wanna play Beavis and Butthead.

"You know the fuck this is. Where my money? I loan you that shit like some months ago. Where my money, nigga?!" I'on really want it but I hate his ass dat much.

"Bitch, you ain't said shit."

I know dis nigga not swelling threats.

I jump in my other truck, hit I-95 thinking wit' a smile on my face, just knowing what I'ma do to dis nigga if he don't have my greenbacks. I pull into the lot where Classics night club used to be.

I see my crew positioned but no Eric in sight. He told me to meet him here. *Where that bama nigga at dough?*

"I know dis joka ain't tryna feel the heat for real?" I say to myself.

Ten minutes later I see headlights shining on my truck. *Pow! Pow! Pow! Pow!*

Bullets flying from everywhere, then tires spin, screeching out the parking lot. I call out to my boy who's looking on—he doesn't shoot, doesn't even give chase. We know who the culprit is. I laugh. *Good thing my truck bulletproof.* I'm mad 'cause I won't get ta see that nigga die tonight. I ride out wit' my crew. My cell blows up.

"Yo," I answer. It's my man Midget.

"Get this man. I just saw Eric at the gamble house."

"Oh yeah, I'm there."

That nigga ain't even think to hit my tires. Stupid fuck, I'm thinking as I pull up to the gamble house. I get out, wave for 3 of my killas to come in wit' me. The others stay on lookout. We go in, I scan the joint, no Eric—but I see dis ugly nigga eyeballing me. I walk his way, he takes off running, we give chase, catching up wit' his bony ass out back. I grab'em by his little ass neck, throw'em on the ground.

"What you running fo', partna?"

"It wasn't' me!" I swear dis nigga starts crying for real.

"Yes it was. I saw you," I lie 'cause I don't know what the fuck he talkin 'bout.

"No, it was James. He said he killed him."

My ears on blast. "James killed him? Why?" I'm still playing the tape all the way through but still lost.

"He said Andrew ordered the hit. We had to do it or die."

"Oh, he did? Ok, I understand man. So tell me more." I'm still lost.

"Zecman, if I tell you, can I be down wit' you? Wit' y'all?"

"Hell yeah," I tell'em, lying.

"Ok, Ok. I left him to brush off his shit. We walk back inside, take a seat at the makeshift bar. I order him a drink to loosen his green ass up a bit."

"Tell me what you know. I got you, no worries."

"He killed Kurt. Then he put the order out to kill your wife."

"My wife?"

"Yes." He nods his head, downing his drink, looking like Andy Griffin. "He said if we didn't try to kill'a, he was gon' kill us and our family."

"When I saw you kill Murry Boonman and lil Squirt I know you was coming for me next. But it wasn't them; it was James. He killed yo sister and took your daughter."

My dick jumps. *I gotta kill'em. Dis nigga so Jelly of me for fucking his wife, he after raw blood. I neva knew he was the one. I got some'em fo' his ass. I know he ride kill'a blood but it's kill or be killed at this point. I already got James punk ass, now I gotta go get Andrew's too. This gon' be war between me and Chance, then so be it. For now I gotta see Andrew. No exceptions, I got to.*

Chapter 44

Zec's right hand, Lil Man

"Man, this joint smokin'. What y'all do up in here, trick off?" Eric's punk ass hollas, grabbing the play station handles taking a seat.

"Yeah man some'em like dat. Look, sit over here in this chair. It's more comfy," I insist.

"Ok, Ok." He follows directions wit' his happy go lucky ass. "I'm so—"

Bloc! Bloc!

"Shut the fuck up. Damn," I say, lookin' down at his lame ass body. "I'm so glad Zec wasn't fo' real 'bout you gettin' down with the crew. If he was, I would've just had'ta break the code and kill yo ass anyway. Talk too fuckin much, fo' real."

I call Zec. "Hey," he answers.

"Them ribs BBQ'd nicely," I spit.

"Did you clean the grill good?" he inquires.

"Already on it."

"I hear dat." He laughs.

"I'll meet up wit' you tomorrow. We got work ta do."

"You know I love my pay," I remind his ass, ending the call.

Chapter 45
Deja

I leave the visit room, run to my unit looking for Pee. I spot a few of her buddies playing spades.

"Trish, you seen Pee?"

"Nah," she says all uppity as shit.

I spot this old Gee who looks like an old ass man. She's playing Pinochle.

"Pop, you seen Pee?"

"Last time I saw'a she was at the Rec. Why?" Pop asks.

Ignoring her nosy ass, I head out for the Rec, jogging up to the door.

I look around, no Pee. I go to the track. My head is moving from right ta left. I'm on fire. I spot'a talking ta a group of hoes. I jog up to'a. She looks at me like, *What in the entire fuck is up wit' you?*

"What's up? You look flexed," she notices.

"Flex ain't the word," I pump back.

"I'ma get wit' y'all later," she tells them hoes.

"Can you believe dat nigga got a son?"

"A what? Who we talkin' 'bout?" She's lost.

"My bad, Zec."

"Dang Ma, sorry," she consoles. "Look, don't be stressing. Ain't nutten you can do. Shawdy, you got time in front of yo ass. Feel dat shit and only dat."

"Fuck time."

"Listen, who he got the son by? Do you know'a?" Pee yawps.

"I know it's that fuckin April. I can't believe this shit. Out of everything people told me about him this right here beats the cake."

"April? The dead chick? Lil man needs one parent, right?" She hard looks my ass. Like I'm the one in the wrong.

I spot check her ass back like she lost her mind.

She throws up her hands like, *What you want me to say?*

"I'm getting outta here soon. When I do, I'ma kill his ass."

"Really? Really, D? You know how the game's played. You been wit' a gangsta for like years. Dis shit ain't knew, so what you trippin' on? Zec being him, what you allowed him to do all these years. You in here; it ain't shit you can do 'bout it, so now you mad? Slow down. Think, shawdy, think. You'on want my time for real. Dat nigga gon' play the

same way he was playing when you was out there in the free world," she stresses.

"I'm tripping on him having a son close to the fuckin age as our daughter he ain't tell me. We don't keep secrets. That shit's for punk ass relationships. I know he was fuckin April but a 13 year-old-son? Really fuckin really?!" I spit, crossing my arms over my chest.

"D, get a grip. You talking out your head right now. You mad."

"Fuck calm. He playing house while I sit in here. Over my fuckin dead ass body!" I yell, then walk away with a bright ass idea. I go to my unit, walk in my cell, grab hold of my phone book off my locker. I wait for the damn phone 'cause they full.

"Come on y'all ain't talkin 'bout shit. Get off the phone," I say out loud, wanting them to hurry. I bite my nails, standing, waiting, listening to these hoes talk about absolutely nothing. One girl hangs up.

I walk to the phone, passing her.

"We all get a chance," she says, directing it to me. I let her have it, got other shit on my brain right now.

Dialing the number on the card in my hand, "Please state your name at the tone," the machine says.

"Deja Colman," I speak into the phone.

"Deja Colman," the machine repeats.

The phone rings.

"Hello?"

"Hello, you have a prepaid call from a federal prisoner, *Deja Colman*. This call will be recorded. If you want to accept this call, press 5. If you do not want to accept a call like this press 7. To end this call, hang up."

"I hate this damn phone."

"Hello?"

"Is my attorney there?" I get straight to the fuckin point.

"Yes. Hold on, Mrs. Colman," the receptionist says.

After one minute or so, "Deja, how are you?"

"Good. Look, I got 3 bodies for the FBI. 3," I tell'em.

"Whoo what?"

"3 bodies. I'll give them the location if they let me."

"They will ask who and how, you know."

"Fine wit' me. They been tryna solve the fuckin murders so I'll solve it fo they stupid asses."

"Ok, I'll be there. Let me see … how about Thursday? That's 4 days from today. We can talk then. I'll call the attorney general."

"Fine by me," I tell him.

"Why now?" he asks.

"My daughter."

"I'll see you next week."

"Good," I say and hang up.

A *Classy* THUG

"This nigga wanna fuck wit' me. He wanna get monkey wit' my ass. I'ma feed him monkey nuts and make'em eat dat shit, ole bitch!" I say out loud, hanging up the phone.

I'm a pissed off bitch!

Chapter 46

Zec

I lay in the bed, getting some TV time. Jus climbs in wit' me.

Scooting down under the covers into my arms, "Z, what you know about me?"

That shit comes from nowhere.

"Huh?"

"What you know about me?" she asks again.

Lifting up wit' my elbow on the bed, resting my head on my hand, rubbing her belly, I look down at her.

"You love seafood, all kinds. Your favorite color is red but you like black cars like your man. You like being alone in the mornings to read the newspaper to drink your coffee. Oh your coffee you like that black too. Your hobby is riding go-carts. You also like to go to the dog races on Sunday so you can spend time wit' your father. You love children, you like dogs; Pit bulls is your choice. Blue nose Pits at that. You love drawing and poetry, you have a PHD in economics. But most of all you love me. You'll do any and er' thing to make sure I'm happy. However, it's nothing you won't do to make your daddy happy. Am I right?" I ask wit' a soft grin on my face, drawing circles around her navel wit' my finger.

She returns the smile. "I love you, Z."

"I love you too."

Lifting up, she reaches for the drawer of the night stand. "What you doing, bae?" Not another toilet I hope.

She hands me a box.

"You don't have to keep buying me stuff. I have like fifty watches," I exclaim.

"I know but this one is special. So open it."

Holding the black square box, I open it. "What, what's dis 'bout?" I ask, shocked for the first time in my life.

She has that glow in her eyes.

"Wow! Jus, don't I supposed to be doing the purposing?"

"Boy, this the 20th century."

"I see. 25 diamonds around this band. It's hot, bae."

"You worth every one of them."

"Now you got a nigga feeling like a bitch," I tell'a, taking the ring from the box, placing it on my ring finger.

I look at her wit' a big ass grin. "How you know my ring size?"

"I didn't. I asked Nikki to get it from you."

"So that's why she asked me how big my fingers were, one by one? So she's in on the conspiracy wit' yo ass? See, that's how it all goes down. That's how niggaz get 20 years conspiracy," I joke.

She takes my hand. "Zecman, will you marry me?"

"Umm, let me see."

Her eyes pop out the membranes.

"I'm playing." She hits me on my arms. I laugh. "Yes, I knew you would be my wife from the first day we met."

We kiss, a passionate kiss from somewhere I've never been. Then we make love into the night, cow girl love. She rides the whole time. For some reason I'm not a minute man wit' her.

Chapter 47
Deja
Three Days Pass

"Hey mamma," Nikki says.

"Hey to you, baby girl. How is things going?" I ask her.

"Fine, ma. Are you gon' be out in time for daddy's wedding?"

"His wedding?"

"Yep, he gettin' married in 2 months. You told me you was working on something to get you home to me."

"I am. Where is he getting married?" The hell with what Nikki's talkin 'bout me getting out. I need to know where his ass was betraying me at.

"Outside at the Potomac Park. It's going to be huge. 400 people. And I'm in the wedding, the maid of honor." She seems so excited.

"You are?" I feed her.

"Yep. And Jr. is the best man. It's 20 people on each side. We been practicing."

"Boy, that's nice. So you like her?"

"Yeah, she's really nice," she tells me. My fuckin heart sinks. I continue my line of questioning.

"Nikki, you're going to be a blessed child. You'll have two mommies."

"I know but I'm already blessed. I have you, momma."

Now that makes me feel better. I love her.

"When is the date?"

"June 10th," she informs me.

"You wanna talk to Auntie? 'Cause Jr. and me getting ready to go to the movies with Jus and daddy."

Fuck, I gotta get the fuck outta here. Chance ain't come through yet, nor has my lawyer. What is going on? I think to myself.

"That's her name?" I get back on track.

"Yes, it's Juswa. But she said we can call her Jus."

"Jus it is."

"Jus wants to meet you but she said she'll wait until you get home. She's white, mamma." I liked ta chock this mother fucka messing wit' a white bitch. My ears steaming. I can't hear no more, I might commit suicide.

"Nikki, you have fun ok? I love you."

I hang up the phone, sick. I rush to the table. I see Pee and Tic sitting watching TV. I tell'em what my daughter just told me in detail. The frown on Pee's face says it all.

A *Classy* THUG

"I could've told you she was white," Tic interjects, even though I was talking to Pee.

My ass is puzzled as I look over at her.

"You talkin 'bout the guy that came to visit you not too long ago, right?" she adds.

I nod. "I seen him bundled up wit' a snow bunny at the basketball game a minute ago before I got locked up. I thought you knew. I saw him, your daughter—well the girl that comes to see you—and another lil boy that looks just like him. The lil boy so cute. I couldn't help but remember him."

"Why you ain't say shit?"

"Girl, I'on get in people business. And like I said, I thought you knew."

"I can respect that," I tell her.

"You can't do nutten but respect that," Pee adds.

"What she look like, Tic?" I need to know.

"You really wanna know?" she asks.

"I asked, didn't I?"

"Ok, she looks mixed wit' some'em. She's not just white. More Italian, really long thick blond and black hair, like a size E breast. Fake, perfect round ass—well it looks fake, never know. Hazel eyes. She's fine as shit. I'ing gon' lie, she on point." Pee gives her a *you didn't have 'ta cut her throat* look. "I mean she ok, you're pretty too," she adds, trying to make me feel better.

"It's ok. If she's got looks, she's got looks. I'ma go swallow this shit. I'll holla at y'all two love birds later."

"You gon' be ok?" Pee asks.

"I'm Gucci," I tell her, frontin'. 'Cause my feelings on straight break down.

Chapter 48

Zec

Months Pass

"Boy, my nerves on edge," I tell my man Tiny while looking in the body length mirror, fixing my tie.

"I'm wit' you on that one. Ain't neva been married, won't ever be married," he assures himself, sipping on some Crown.

"This mean no mo' on the road pussy for real," I tell'em, still tryna fix this damn tie.

"'Eva," he spits back, sitting at the table of my trailer.

"Man, thanks for the wedding gift. Fo' different Islands. See, normal people would've picked one but you went all out man. Thanks," I tell his ass.

"Man, what you give a multi-millionaire on his wedding day?" He laughs.

"'Point made."

"I could have gotten you a chess game but ..." His voice travels off.

"Now you got jokes," I tell his ass.

"You remember, huh?" he reflects.

"Do I? Like it was last night. That was funny. Dad got married, you handed him his gift, telling him to open it up. He did and it was a fuckin chess board. He looked at you like you had four eyes. We all bust out laughing. Dat joint was so funny. Til dis day it's still funny."

"It was the meaning. I wanted him to learn the game so he would know how to survive in life wit'out me."

He drifts again. I turn, tie still not on point.

"It's ok, man. He's with us today. He's with us I'm sure," I coach.

He holds his glass up. I walk over to him, placing my hand on his shoulder.

"Man, it's cool. I know, I miss my old man too. He got what it meant. He just got sloppy, that's all. But I'm here."

He looks up at me, dropping caskets. "Z man, watch yo back 'cause I'm too damned old to watch it for you. Treat Jus good. Treat her like she's yo side woman, your mistress, give her the world, don't let nothing or no one come between y'all. If you claim you love her, show her. Talk is cheap. Take her everywhere you go. Most of all have respect for her, the same you have for your kids."

When he said that last line my heart jumped, then I drop a casket or two. He stands, showing me some love. For some reason I didn't wanna break our embrace. It felt like my father was in him.

Chapter 49

Juswa

"Girl, it's your day," my friend Penny confirms.

"Yes, it is. My day alone."

We laugh.

"I gotta give it to ya. This one is fine as hell. He's too buff for me but damn 6'6", about 280 in weight, cream color skin, curly black hair. Oh my God. I know you be running your nails through it. Who wouldn't, right? Yo man's lips so big. I would die every night if Paul had lips like that. Wait, and his butt—it's so perfect, like your fake butt. Talking about fake butts, I need to see Jason so he can give me some more injections. Paul would die if my butt shrinks. You know how black men love them some butt anyway. Have you done any S&M on him Madam?"

My head turns around like the exorcist. "No!" I snap. "He doesn't know about that and he never will. So never mention it again," I order, sitting, getting my makeup applied.

Her mouth is wide open. "So what he think you do?"

"I told him it's all daddy's money."

"Jus, why did you lie? He's a dope boy, why would he care? He's just like your father. Your whole relationship is a lie anyway. Your daddy put you up to all of it. I'm so happy we don't have to follow him around anymore. Boy I'm so glad that's over. I started feeling like inspector Reno. I was so happy he finally noticed you at that damn beach 'cause Key West wasn't the spot for me. I love New York," she tells me, filing her nails. "Anyway, why your father want you with him?"

I roll my eyes. She works my patience. I excuse my makeup artist for a minute. When she leaves the room, "My father and his father were partners. His father left his part of the company to his son. Which happens to be Z. Z can't get the other half of the company until he gets married so, *voilà*—it will stay in the family, our family. I will sign the company over to my father. You don't really think I love him, do you? Penny, he's not my type. Satan is. Now I would've married his ass for free. Daddy's paying me 4 million to marry his ass. Bitch wake up. Get wit' the program," I deliver.

"He's not that bad though. He's a handsome man that knows how to get his own money. That's more than I can say for most. Satan, he's a thug, a outward thug, a real killer acting thug. Who wants that?"

A *Classy* THUG

"Me. He turns me on. But hear this: Z killed his ex-girlfriend, who his son is by. He killed his father too. Girl, his own father." I move away from my makeup chair and sit beside her.

"What?!" She screams, putting her hand over her mouth.

"Yeah, my jaw dropped too. He don't know I know but dad told me. His father owed Calvin money, one of my dad's business partners. Zec was the hitman for my father back then. He was only like in his teens or something like that. Dad handed Zec the address of his next job. I remember standing on the steps, looking over the rails as I always did. I saw Zec's face. He looked at my father who was stone face and nodded his head. The next day Zec's dad, the man I called Uncle Lou, was on the news. They said she was dead. I was young but that I remember 'cause Zec the only boy that work for my dad that was so close to my age so I took notice."

"Oh my heavens, Jus. And you're marrying the man?"

I call my makeup artist back in, going back to my chair.

"Child, he's a little bear cub. He would never hurt me 'cause I'm not dumb enough to step in his path. I give him what he wants—love and hot pussy. He's wealthy." I smile. "He just don't know it. He's going to be filthy rich soon. I'll just be good ole wifey while spending all his money, doing what I do with Satan."

"I'm glad I'm not you, is all I can say. That man gon' kill you and send Satan back to hell if he finds out," she voices.

"I'm done," my makeup artist says.

"Jus, I still say all money isn't good money," my friend reminds me the facts of life.

"Whatever. Come help me with this dress," I demand, picking up my all white $300,000 wedding gown.

As she helps me with my dress, I continue to tell her how he is.

She makes faces, moans, but she is loving the gossip.

Chapter 50
Zec

"Mr. Washington, it's show time," the wedding planner walks into my trailer announcing. "You and your son are going to walk down the aisle side by side just the way we practiced it last night," she reminds me.

"I got you. Where is he?"

"He's on the way to your trailer now."

"Thanks," I reply. "A'ight, Tiny, it's my time ta shine," I say, putting down my drink.

I meet up with Jr. Tiny goes ahead to the stage. Me and Jr. stand at the end of the tent until we hear the song, "A Ribbon in the Sky." My heart turns up one hunnit.

"There's a lot of people in there," I whisper to Jr.

"I know but I got your back, pops." He's growing up fast now that he's wit' me.

"Lil me, when you say pops it gives me some purpose," I let him know.

He smiles.

We walk down the aisles. All eyes on us. I get to the makeshift stage, stand waiting. *I'll be glad when dis shit is over. I need a drink, damn.*

Her music starts to play. Lil girls walk down the aisle, putting flowers down for my baby to walk on and she's worth it too. Then they roll out the red carpet. People are taking pics like paparazzi. My lovely Nikki walks down with flowers in her hand. *Man, she's so beautiful. She looks just like Deja. She didn't get none of my looks. My lil daughter,* I think to me.

"We've only just begun" fills the air. More flashes go off. People stand. My bride pops up. She starts walking down toward me. She's the prettiest woman I've ever seen. She looks like she belongs on the cover of a magazine. *Damn, only if I loved her like Deja. Only if Deja had her qualities. Marrying Jus will guarantee me a spot on her father's team, something I wanted all my life.*

I know I can't be a mob Boss. I don't have their blood. I can run shit, all the companies, er' thing. Tiny didn't have ta tell me ta treat her like a queen. I know the game. I plan on playing it well, even though I do wish dat was Deja coming down the fuckin aisle to our favorite song.

She gets to the stage. I help her up.

"You're beautiful," I whisper.

"And you're stunning," she replies.

A *Classy* THUG

I hold her hand. The preacher does his thing. Her father gives her away to me.

Then I hear, "I now pronounce you man and wife. You may kiss the bride."

I lean in to kiss my bri—"

Boom! Click-clack, Boom! Click-clack, Boom! Click-clack, Boom!

It sounds like shots from er where. The crowd's screaming; it's chaos! I hit the ground, taking Jus wit' me. I look to my right for Nikki. I don't see'a; then left for Jr. He's on the ground. I scan the park.

Is that Deja wit' a black hoodie, standing wit' a sawed off lowered by her side between them trees? She's looking right at me. She lowers her hoodie so I can get a good look at'a. She missed me on purpose. I know 'cause that bitch got aim. I taught'a. What seems like hours is only minutes. She turns, walks into the dark of the woods.

People still run, car engines starting up, they getting ghost. I run to my son, lifting him up by his arm, scanning for blood. *None, good.*

"You ok?" I ask.

He nods. He's shaking.

I scan for Nikki.

"Daddy, daddy." She runs up to me, hugging me around my waist.

I look back at my new wife. I lift her up. She's limp, blood er' where. I look in the front for her father. He's laying in a pool of blood, his two hangmen dead, heads blown off. I dial 911 for Jus. I can feel her heart beating faintly.

"Jus, the police on the way, stay wit' me, baby. I need this. I need you to stay wit' me. Don't fuck this up. I waited fo' dis too long, my family's future depends on it. Come on now, stay wit' me." I'm applying pressure on the hole of her back.

The ambulance gets here, thank God. They jump out their truck, doing all they can for er' body. I look over my shoulders.

"Tiny, take the kids. I'll meet you at my crib. Here's the keys." I throw them to'em. "Y'all go with unc Tiny. I'll see you in a minute, Jr." I kiss them both, sending them off wit' my man.

When the police arrive they ask questions. I answer the best I can. When they're done, I head for my ride. Opening the door I hop in, only to notice a black rose attached to a note on my windshield. Reaching my arm around, I grab the shit, throwing the rose on the ground, reading the note.

You killed my mother. I killed your dreams. Signed the wife that should've been.

Chapter 51

Zec

One Week Later

I'm sitting here watching my wife hooked up to all these cords and machines.

"I can't believe Deja did all dis damage. What in the cow fuck was she thinking?" I say in a low voice to me.

"Hello, Mr. Washington."

"Hello, Doc. What's the word?" I need to know.

"She's a fighter. It's only been a week. We have to pray, give it some time. As I said, the bullet entered through her upper back but it traveled quickly, stopping at her heart. If we try to remove it, it may have traveled. She would not be here today."

"But she's not. The machine is keeping her alive."

"So it seems. Mr. Washington, she's doing a lot of the work as well. Just pray, Sir," he tells me.

"How long can she live like this?"

"Until she decides to wake up, or whenever you decide to say no more."

"I'll never pull the cord. She's my wife."

"I understand. I was just answering your question. I'm in the middle of making rounds. I'll see you tomorrow, I guess. Just pray," he says again, patting me on my arm as he leaves the room.

Standing over her body looking down at her soft skin, her lovely face, "Baby, you've got to make it. My family has to own the cities. I need your voice to take over your father's empire, to get what my father left me. Yeah, I know all about it. It was in the back of my mind when you asked me to marry you. I do my homework. It's ok. I fell in love with you through it all." I bend over, placing my lips on her face. When I lift up, I see the big boys coming my way. I already told them I don't know shit. They entered her room.

"Mr. Washington?"

"That's me."

"You're under arrest"—they start putting handcuffs on me—"for the murders of Mr. Copeland, Squirt; Mr. Rolando, Boons; Mr. Seaman, Mury; and Eric Colman."

"What? Murder? I ain't never murder nobody. You got the wrong man. I was at my wedding. What you talking 'bout?" I lie.

"You can explain yourself downtown."

"Can I kiss my wife bye?"

A *Classy* THUG

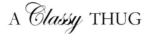

"You already did when you killed somebody else's husband."

They walk my ass out the hospital. The doctor I was just talking to, he's standing in the hall looking with the other staff.

As I pass him, "Doc, take care of her. Don't let her die. This just a misunderstanding. I'll be back!" I yell, thinking, *Only two people knew about them niggaz. One is dead, that's my man Kurt, and the other is Deja. That bitch, she got me. That bitch. To think I was doing all this for her and our family. Then the other, Eric, only Lil man knew about that shit! I know his ass ain't double cross me and shit!*

Chapter 52
Errica

Man, this what I call the life. All I been doing is tricking people to give up their children. Dropping drugs in their drinks after I fuck they asses. I been getting paid. I'm living high on a hog. Andrew ass is under me know. I'm Chance's right hand bitch. Andrew don't even know what's going on in the day to day operation. All he is, is a go-get boy that watches over the crew. After I found out he like to fuck sheep in the ass, I never let Drew fuck me again. Fuckin sheep, that's some ole West, VA shit right there.

I love this shit, I say to myself, fixing up my condo on the waterfront of Fort Washington, Maryland, 12th floor.

All I do is go out like five times a month, that's it. Then I enjoy my life gambling, running the streets doing me. I have a bitch now, 'cause men—they ain't shit. I take care of her 24-7. She don't want fo' shit. She's a boy-girl; that's how

I like'em. She kinda remind me of a man. She's even got a goatee.

"My love, what you doing sitting out here all by yourself?" she walks in and asks.

"Just taking in the view," I respond as she kisses me down my soft body, stopping at my kitty cat. "Yes, baby, right there. Take care yo bitch," I tell'a.

Chapter 53
Deja

Now see how you like that shit, you son of a muthafucking biscuit. You wanna kill my mother, my fuckin mother who's been there for you when you didn't have shit. When your mother died she let you in. Your father died, she was there for you. She raised your 2 brothers as hers. Paid for your sista to go to college. You bitch, how could you kill my mother? Then my brother too. Fuck you.

Then yo ass wanna play family wit' my daughter and another bitch, a white bitch at dat. I should've dropped yo ass too. Humph, I rather see you suffer. It's better that way, I vent to me while putting dishes in the dishwasher, still vexed about that shit. I walk out on the terrace of our vacation home.

"Here, baby. Your drink."

"I was missing you. What was you doing in there?"

"I was putting dishes in the wash machine, thinking about life."

"Let me do the thinking for you now. You mines now. You don't have to do shit but love me, take care of the things you love to do, that's it. We're a family now."

J.J. Jackson

I sit between his legs watching Nikki play on the beach with her new dog. He kisses me on the nape of my neck, causing me to blush.

"Chance, I'm so glad you know. I'm so glad it was you that sent Satan to me undercover. I'm so happy we're together. I love you so much. Thanks for getting me out that God forsaken place. What would I have done without you? The Feds was talking about keeping me in there for 2 more years, even with the information I gave them."

"I told you not to do it. I was gon' get you out. You didn't have faith in your man?"

"I do now. I just wish you would tell me what it is you do to afford all the nice stuff you do for me and Nikki, all the places we've been so far."

"I told you a man's business is his alone. All you have to worry about is me taking care of you and Nikki. Next week I'm taking you to my Gana's country so you can meet my family, you and Nikki."

"I can't wait," I tell'em.

He licks his chops. "I can't either."

His cell rings. "Hello? Baby, I gotta take this," he says, lifting me up off him to go inside.

I'm not trippin' 'cause I know it's business and if it wasn't he respecting me so much that he don't lead me to think he fucking wit' other women. I love it.

Chapter 54
Chance

"Hey, man, what it be like?"

"Nutten, man. Did you get the package from Satan?" I ask him.

"Oooh yeah. I was just sending some love yo way. You kept your word."

"Ain't no other way to live. Thanks for lacing them boys' ears with that news," I say.

"No doubt. Anything else you need me to do for you, just holla. Nigga you pay well."

"I'll keep you on speed dial."

"Again, thanks man. Much respect," Lil man repeats.

"Again, you're welcome. I'll holla if I need more work."

"Holla," he says, ending our call.

"Dirty niggaz. I would never again get at his ass. He's a rat. What won't a nigga do for money? He betrayed his own man."

I dial my sister in Vietnam.

"Hello?"

"Sis, did you line everything up? Did you get the house I asked you to get?"

"Yes, Chance. You know I did. When are they coming?"

"I'm bringing them next week. I won't be staying long, just for like one month at a time. I'm dropping them off."

"Suppose she don't wanna stay."

"She don't have a choice. I'm gon' marry here, bring her there then take their passports. How she gon' get back? You just treat her good. If she don't wanna stay I know her organs will make a match with somebody's. All I need is my daughter."

"I can't wait to meet my niece. I love you, brother. I'm excited."

"Same here. I'll see you soon."

I end the call.

Now that I have shawdy, she'll never get away from me again.

I walk back on the terrace to see her playing with our daughter. I smile. This is what family feels like. *Finally, my own family.*

I run out to join them on the beach. We take turns throwing the Frisbee to one another, then the dog. We all laugh, enjoying the day. This is what I call life. Doing shit the

A *Classy* THUG

ole classic way—a dog, wife, child; it don't get bedda than that. And I'm sending them where no one can get to them, to get to me. Ain't life sweet?

The following is an excerpt from J.J. Jackson's:

Hell Has No Fury

Chapter 1

It's three in the afternoon. The bells of Howard University's law school rings. Blair slams her law book shut, grabs her book bag, throws it over her shoulder and heads for the door. She walks down the long hallway to the ladies room, rushes to the first available stool. She drops her book and book bag on the floor, hurrying as she pulls her skirt up and her thong to the side. Squatting over the commode, she sighs as she releases the warm fluids that she's been holding ever since class started two hours ago. She wipes and flushes the commode quickly. She exits, washes her hands then races out the restroom. She moves fast, trying not to be late for her next class.

One more class, then home. I'm so damn tired all I can think about is my bed and pillow. They're calling my name, she thinks to herself.

She's so excited to be entering Mr. Parker's financial law class, which happens to be her favorite subject. She's always dreamed of being a CPA, but her mother insisted on her going to law school so she made accounting her minor and Political law her major. Blair's father is the former mayor of Washington DC. Needless to say he's pleased with her choices.

"Glad you could join us," Professor Parker voices, looking straight at Blair as she walks in his classroom. She stops in her tracks, looks around seeing all eyes are on her and this makes her feel a little embarrassed that he put her on blast; after all, she's only ten minutes late. She had to run down two long halls and some steps to get to his class. She remains silent, nods her head then takes a seat.

"Pull out your books and turn to page 180. We will be reading the quotes of Lord Montgomery 1877-1976. He was a British field Marshal. Now does anyone know his famous quote?" the Professor asks as he connects eyes with Blair. "Well Ms ..."

She sees he's talking to her.

"Wilson. Blair Wilson," she states her name.

"Ok, Ms. Wilson."

He pauses. She notices he's waiting for her to answer the question.

"Um ... I mean ... Um," she's hesitant, looking down for her books.

"You forgot something, like your book?" he asks.

Her eyes dart around the room. "Uh no I...I think I left it. No, I mean—"

He cuts her off. "I can see you left it. Hell, Ray Charles can see that," he fires off disrespectfully.

The class starts laughing.

Blair grows embarrassed. She leaps from her chair quickly, walking to the exit door. Once in the hall she rushes back to the restroom where she must have left all her belongings. When she turns the corner that leads to the restroom she bumps someone.

"Excuse me!" she says still moving along. She enters the restroom panicking, looking in all the stalls. "Nothing. Damn all my shit!" she stomps and rubs her temples then walks out the restroom with a look of defeat.

"Excuse me," a gentleman's voice rings out.

"What is it!" she snaps, not looking up.

"I just wanted to know if you know where the chow hall is."

She takes a deep breath, her face softens. "You're in the wrong building."

"Shit, somebody told me it was in this building. Man this place is like a damn maze," he says, looking around.

"I know."

She looks over at the tall sexy six foot seven handsome man that stands before her. She runs her fingers through her long wavy jet black hair, her dark brown eyes softens as her full pink lips flutter. She's never seen a man so fine and sexy all in one so close she could just reach out and touch him.

I thought these type of men were only in magazines.

He notices she is a little flustered. "My bad what's your name?" he asks.

"Blair, and yours?"

"I'm Jerode, but they call me Jazz."

"Ok, Jazz. I see you don't go here so what school do you go to. That is if you go to school?" she asks with a smirk.

"Nah, I'm a George Towner."

Her head snaps back, her eyebrows rise to attention. "Oh really? So what's your major?" She's impressed.

He smiles. "Basketball."

Go figure I knew he couldn't have the brains to fine, she's thinking still admiring his looks.

"That's not a major."

"Well, it's one to me. But I take accounting."

Wow I like'em already.

"And you do go here?" he asks.

"Yep," she answers proudly.

"You just hanging out?" Seeing she has not one book in hand, he looks her up and down. She notices.

"I left my books. Oh forget it," she says, waving her hand in the air.

"So what's your major?"

"Political law and—"

He cuts her off. "It's more? I mean anything wit' the word politic in it and law is enough, ain't it?" he jokes.

"You're funny, really funny. My major is Political law but my minor is Accounting. I want to be a Certified Public Accountant one day."

"Well why didn't you just make that your major and be done wit' it, or are you one of them girls that's living out their family's dreams?"

"Never," she lies.

"Look, we having a party tonight at the House of Colors … if you wanna come?"

"Sure, why not. Sounds like fun," she answers with a big smile on her face.

"Good do you know where it is?" he asks.

"Uh duh, who don't?" she says, rolling her eyes.

He glances at his watch. "Ok bet. I gotta meet somebody in the chow hall. I'm late as it is, and she is gon' be pissed, but such is life."

"She? So you're meeting your girl?" she boldly put out there.

"You jelly?" He smiles, showing his pearly whites.

"Jelly! Boy I don't even know you like that!"

"You wanna get to know me like that?"

"You got jokes," she tells him.

"Nah it's my sister she goes here."

"Oh."

"Yeah oh, but I'll see you tonight at ten. That is if your momma lets you out past dark," he says with a chuckle.

"Ok, Steve Harvey. Ten it is," she adds, blushing as she watches his sexy ass turn and head the opposite way.

She's so caught up with Jazz she almost forgot she lost all her belongings, then it hits her. She heads to the lost and found, hoping someone was kind enough to turn her stuff in.

But she can't get Jazz off her mind.

Text **JORDAN** to **77948**

And stay updated on all of Jordan Belcher Presents' *newest releases, free giveaways,* and *special promotions!*

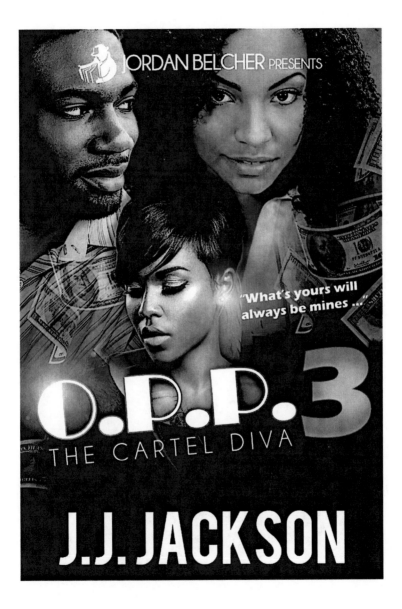

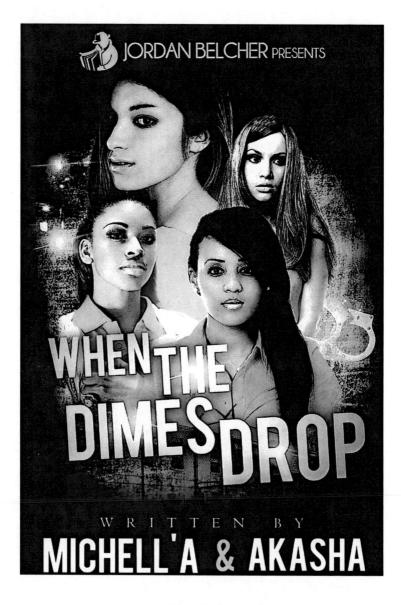

ON SALE NOW!

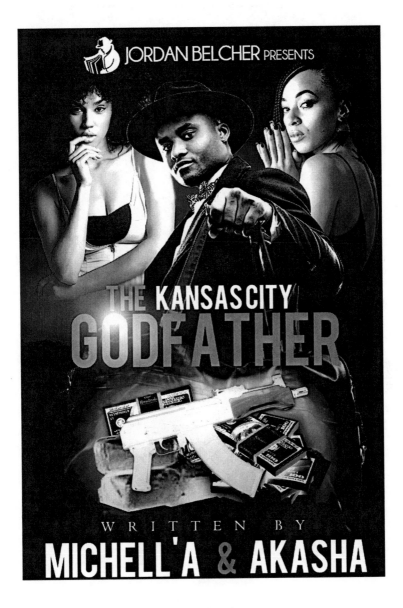

ON SALE NOW!

CPSIA information can be obtained
at www.ICGtesting.com
Printed in the USA
LVOW10s1727020817
543567LV00002B/223/P